To the holder of this letter,

My commendations. Solving the puzzle of the chest required more than considerable deductive powers.

My work has consumed my life, and I have produced no heir to follow in my path. But I picture you: a young man of good imagination.

Any mystery devised by mortal minds can be solved therewith.

Yours faithfully,

Sherlock Holmes

Other Yearling Books You Will Enjoy:

YEARLING BOOKS are designed especially to entertain and enlighten young people. Patricia Reilly Giff, consultant to this series, received her bachelor's degree from Marymount College and a master's degree in history from St. John's University. She holds a Professional Diploma in Reading and a Doctorate of Humane Letters from Hofstra University. She was a teacher and reading consultant for many years, and is the author of numerous books for young readers.

THE CASE OF THE BURNING BUILDING and THE CASE OF THE RUBY RING

by Judie Angell

A Yearling Book

Published by
Bantam Doubleday Dell Books for Young Readers
a division of
Random House, Inc.
1540 Broadway
New York, New York 10036

Created by Winklemania
Text and art copyright © 1999 by Shirley Productions Inc. and Holmes Film Productions Inc.

Original screenplay for *The Case of the Burning Building* by Susin Nielsen
Original screenplay for *The Case of the Ruby Ring* by Dennis Foon

Visit us on the Web! www.randomhouse.com
Educators and librarians, for a variety of teaching tools, visit us at
www.randomhouse.com/teachers

ISBN: 0-440-41500-4

Printed in the United States of America

March 1999

10 9 8 7 6 5 4 3 2 1

OPM

THE CASE OF THE BURNING BUILDING

CHAPTER

Thump!

Shirley opened her eyes. She was a light sleeper, and the slightest sound usually woke her.

She knew *that* sound, though. That was the paperboy tossing his morning delivery at the front door. And he was early! She could tell because of the faint pink glow of dawn from the window, instead of the usual bright streak of light across her blanket.

"Six-thirty," she whispered, and then checked her alarm clock.

"Well . . . close." She smiled to herself. "Six twenty-five."

Twelve-year-old Shirley pushed her long brown hair away from her pretty face and bounced out of bed. She threw on a bathrobe, tiptoed down the hall so as not to wake her father, and hurried down the long staircase to the front door. But before she could pull it open, a bud snore startled her. She turned quickly to find her large brown-and-white basset hound sound asleep on the hearth rug in front of the living room fireplace. Smiling, she went over to give him a pat and a hug.

"Watson," she whispered, "what are you doing down here so early?" She got up and headed for the door again. "The newspaper's here, Watson," she told him as she opened it. "Want to come with me and see what's up?"

The dog's answer was another snore. He waggled his long ears and went back to sleep.

Shirley laughed softly and, clutching the paper, ran back up the stairs.

Her grandmother had a small apartment all to herself in the Holmeses' big house, and it was there Shirley headed. Gran would be long gone, Shirley knew. She was either at the park or at the Rec Center doing her exercises. Tai Chi kept her young, Gran insisted. She kept trying to interest Shirley in it, but her granddaughter's interest came and went.

Shirley pushed open the door of Gran's sitting room. Just to the right and next to the big bay window was a bookcase that went from ceiling to floor. Shirley pushed a tiny button on one of the shelves, and with a soft *whoosh*, the bookcase revolved, stopped, and was suddenly an open door leading to another staircase. This one was steeper and harder to climb, but Shirley was up in an instant.

This was Shirley's *real* room: the one where she spent much of her time at home.

It was part of the house's attic. Shirley had organized all her things, but to a stranger it would look like chaos and clutter. There were old steamer trunks with leather and brass latches, books and more books, piles of newspapers, bottles and jars, mysterious wood and stone carvings.

On the wall above an old overstuffed chair hung a portrait of a man. His clothing was not modern; he seemed to be attired in some sort of dark cape, and on his head he wore a tweed cap with earflaps. In his right hand he held a large pipe with a curved stem. But it was his eyes one saw first. The artist had captured the eyes of a man who seemed to look right through you, a man who knew and understood your deepest secrets.

Shirley smiled at the portrait and gave the man a small, brisk salute. Then she turned her attention to her special corner of the room, which contained a small scientific laboratory, a high-tech computer, a printer, and a fax machine. She sat down at her desk, pulled her bathrobe tighter around her, and opened the paper. Her eyes scanned the headlines, flicking from one to another. Suddenly one article caught her eye.

"Police Baffled by String of Arsons," she read, and frowned. Still reading, she reached into the top drawer and removed a pair of scissors, her eyes glued to the story.

"Shirley!" The voice at the foot of the stairs startled her, though it was, as usual, sweet and cheery.

"Be right down, Gran," Shirley called back. Quickly

she clipped the article from the newspaper and folded it into quarters. Her school backpack was propped up against her desk, and she grabbed for it. Into a side pocket she slid the article, then stuffed the rest of the bag with her equipment: a Swiss Army knife, a large magnifying glass, various-sized plastic bags, latex gloves, two plastic shower caps, a surgical mask, and a small kit containing powder and brushes. Checking the clock on the wall, she gasped at the time. Her bathrobe whirled like a cape as she rushed for the door. "Not even dressed yet!" she mumbled to herself. On the first step she stopped. "Rats!" she cried, and went back for her schoolbooks.

Shirley's grandmother was tall and stately-looking, but her twinkling blue eyes showed only warmth and humor. Her hair was a pretty pale blond and curled neatly behind her ears. She smiled to herself as Shirley flew into the kitchen, dressed in her school uniform: plaid skirt, white shirt and striped tie, dark green blazer, dark knee-highs, and brown oxfords.

From his place at the kitchen table, Robert Holmes arched his eyebrow at his daughter. He was a tall, thin, balding man, always neatly dressed. A well-respected diplomat, he worked at the embassy.

"Dressed and ready, eh?" he said to Shirley. "Perhaps you might even make it to school on time today."

"I'll try," Shirley said, and kissed him on the cheek.

"Have some of this, Shirley, dear," Gran offered, as

she poured milk, wheat germ, fruit, and a raw egg into the blender.

"No, thanks, Gran—no time!" Shirley answered, grabbing her lunch bag and an apple from the counter.

"The paper didn't arrive this morning," Shirley's father said, his eyebrow still arched.

"It was early, Dad." Shirley hefted her backpack higher on her back. "I've got it." She pulled it from under the straps of her bag and handed it to him.

"Thank you," he said, and exchanged amused glances with Gran. "Straight to school, now, Shirley," he cautioned.

"You bet, Dad. Bye, Gran! Bye, Watson!" The dog was sprawled across her father's feet, and Shirley bent to pet him before flying out the door.

Mr. Holmes held up the newspaper so that Gran could see the cutout holes. She laughed and shook her head.

CHAPTER  2

There were still wisps and curls of smoke emanating from the gutted building when Shirley arrived. She watched from across the street as a police officer stood guard in front of the yellow tape surrounding the arson site. He shooed some children and a dog away from the area, and Shirley used the moment to cross the street and hide behind a half-collapsed wall.

From her backpack she removed the two shower caps and slipped them over her oxfords. Then she pulled on a pair of latex gloves and her surgical mask and ducked under the yellow tape, which clearly read CRIME SCENE—DO NOT CROSS.

She was very careful as she picked through the rubble and ash.

"Ah," she murmured as something caught her eye. She bent over and examined it closely. "Burned cloth," she whispered. She picked it up and placed it in a small plastic bag. She waded farther into the debris and came upon a small room that had somehow withstood the fire. There! Against the wall . . . what was that? Shirley frowned and crept over.

A pile of rags—not burned, just filthy—and inside, a pair of shabby old sneakers with holes at the toes. The shoes were held together by their laces, tied in a sloppy bow. These were quickly slid into one of Shirley's larger plastic bags.

She checked her watch.

Uh-oh, she thought. But I can still make the second bell if I hurry.

She peeked out from behind a stump of a chimney. The policeman had his back to her; he was still checking the street. *Good*, Shirley thought, and moved toward the door of the little room. As she turned to duck under the yellow tape, she saw something else. It was stuck to the handle of the door. *Gum!* Shirley said to herself. *A wad of gum!* With her Swiss Army knife she scraped it into still another plastic bag.

The policeman suddenly called, "Hey!" and Shirley jumped. But he hadn't seen her. He was trying to roust a homeless man who seemed to be looking for a place to rest.

Shirley began to run down the side street toward the park. It was a shortcut—her school was just at the other end of the woods.

Shirley peeked through the glass in the door of her seventh-grade classroom. The teacher wasn't at the front of the room. *Well, that's a good sign, isn't it?* Shirley thought. She tried to brush off the smudges of ash on her knees, face, and uniform. As quietly as she could, she opened the door. All the students were in their seats and busy writing. Shirley's teacher was at the back of the room near the coat closet, reaching for a book on one of the shelves.

"I can make it," Shirley breathed, and started to tiptoe inside. Her seat was at the front, thankfully.

"Twice in one week, Ms. Holmes!" came a voice from behind her.

Shirley whirled. *Oh, no!* There stood Ms. Stratmann, the school's headmistress.

Shirley opened her mouth but got no chance to speak.

"I think you know what that means, Ms. Holmes. Detention. After school. I'm sure by now you know the time and place! Now you may go and take your seat."

Shirley did, but Ms. Stratmann followed her right into the room, and Shirley noticed for the first time that there was a boy directly behind the headmistress.

He had a lock of straight brown hair that fell over his forehead, and he looked uncomfortable in the school uniform—blue blazer, striped tie, gray trousers. He was scowling.

"Excuse me, class," Ms. Stratmann said. "I would like you to welcome Bo Sawchuk to Sussex Academy." She glanced over at the boy, who looked defiantly at his new fellow students. "I'm sure you'll all do your best to make him feel at home."

The class grew silent and stared back at Bo. He stood still for a moment longer and then strode down an aisle toward an empty seat.

At lunchtime Shirley sat under a tree, staring up at the Sussex Academy building. It was old, stone, and covered with ivy. Shirley knew that many generations of boys and girls whose parents could afford to send them here had passed through its rooms and halls. It was a good school with a fine reputation, and Shirley knew she was fortunate. It was just that . . . there were so many interesting things to see and learn *outside* school, too, and few people seemed to understand that!

She glanced down. Beside her was her unopened lunch bag. She reached for her backpack and removed one of her morning's discoveries: the wad of sooty pink gum in its plastic bag.

When she looked up again, she saw the new boy. What was his name? Bo. Right. Bo Sawchuk. Standing in front of the gardener's shed off to the left, almost hidden by a bush. Actually, he was leaning against it, Shirley noticed, munching on a sandwich. He and she seemed to be the only students having their lunch alone. Bo wasn't looking at her, so she used the time to study him.

As she sat and watched, another boy came around

from the back of the shed. He went right up to Bo and flicked a finger at his tie.

Shirley gathered her things and moved a little closer, without drawing attention to herself.

This boy was bigger and older than Bo. He was wearing jeans and what looked like an expensive leather jacket. He was speaking, but Shirley couldn't hear, so she stood up and began to walk, looking as though she were heading back to the building for class.

"Don't *touch* it, I said!" Bo cried, as he jerked his tie out of the boy's hand.

Some of the students stopped their play and conversation to see what was going on.

"It's nice," the older boy said, smiling. "You look good, all duded up."

"I'm not doin' it," Bo said. He folded his arms and leaned back against the shed.

"Oh, yeah," the boy said menacingly, "you'll do it."

"No way."

"Think of the bread, man," the boy said. "And you know you owe me."

Bo pushed himself away from the shed and started for the school building.

"Don't you walk away from me, man," the boy said, grabbing Bo's arm and pushing him against the shed. The rickety door opened, and Bo fell in.

Some of the students began to edge closer.

Bo jumped up and shoved the bigger boy, who was caught off guard and tripped.

Ms. Stratmann arrived. *"Just what's going on here!"* she bellowed.

The older boy got up quickly and ran behind the shed and toward the woods.

"Mis-ter Sawchuk!" Ms. Stratmann said, glaring at him, her arms folded across her chest. She pointed toward the school. Bo heaved a sigh and began to walk, with Ms. Stratmann close behind him.

Shirley scanned the area, but there was no sign of the other boy.

CHAPTER

The clock on the wall of the administration office read 3:40. Mrs. Fish, the headmistress's secretary, worked at her computer. She had a heavy hand, and her fingernails made a clattering sound on the keyboard. When she turned to make a note on a pad, she wrote hard. Shirley could see her fingers clutching the pencil.

Shirley sighed. She'd been sitting fairly still for forty minutes—some kind of record for her!—and there were still ten minutes to go.

Next to her, in the same sort of chair with a flat, desklike arm for writing, sat Bo Sawchuk. They were the only two in the afternoon's detention period. Bo carefully carved his initials into the arm of his chair with the point of a key while noisily chewing gum.

Shirley touched her lips with her thumb and watched him. He glanced at her briefly and went back to his carving. When he looked up again, she was still watching.

"What's your problem?" he asked sullenly.

"How long have you been in a gang?" Shirley asked.

Bo's eyes widened. "I'm not in a gang," he said, and began to work on his initials again.

"So how come you have that tattoo?" Shirley asked, pointing to his right wrist.

Instinctively Bo's left hand moved to cover it. "Mind your own business," he told her.

Shirley shrugged, and Bo dug his key even harder into the arm of the chair.

"You shouldn't do that," Shirley said. She glanced over at Mrs. Fish, still furiously typing.

"Why, you gonna tell somebody?" Bo asked.

"I wouldn't have to. They're your own initials! Not too smart."

Bo put down the key, embarrassed. "So what are you doing here, anyway? Forget to floss this morning?"

"Tardiness," Shirley told him.

"*Tar-di-ness*," Bo sneered. "What happened, your chauffeur missed a turn or something?"

Shirley opened her hands and indicated her smudged uniform. "If you'd just take a quick look at me, you could tell why I was late. Same way I know that you've never been to private school before, you live on the South Side, you work cleaning fish, and you happen to be color-blind."

Bo's mouth dropped open, but he quickly closed it. "Lucky guesses," he mumbled.

"It's just observation," Shirley said. "For example: You keep tugging at your tie."

"So?"

"If you'd gone to a private school before, a tie would be like a second skin, you'd be so used to it." She pointed to his blazer pocket. "That bus transfer in your pocket: Bus Nine, South Bank. You're wearing one green sock and one blue . . . *and* your skin has a slight residual odor of marine life."

Bo sneaked a sniff of his hand while gaping at Shirley.

Suddenly the clattering of Mrs. Fish's keyboard stopped and she whirled around in her swivel chair.

"Time's up, miscreants," she said with a yawn. She gestured toward the door.

Shirley was up first, grabbed her backpack, and brushed past Bo.

"Hey!" Bo said, and she turned back. "Anyone ever tell you you're weird?"

"Yes," Shirley answered, and was out the door.

CHAPTER

The Shelter for the Homeless was at the end of town near the railroad terminal. Attached to the shelter was an old building that had been, in its day, quite a fashionable restaurant, serving not only the town's elite, but tourists and other visitors as well. Now it was crumbling, propped up by the makeshift carpentry of volunteers and community service workers. But it still had its kitchen and old-fashioned ovens and sinks, and it was now a soup kitchen for the shelter residents and others who were down on their luck.

Shirley was dressed in her after-school clothes, wearing a colorful scarf as a skirt, tights, an embroidered vest, and a multicolored hat. She stepped through the soup kitchen's door. She had her backpack slung over her shoulder, which helped her blend into the crowd. Most of the people there carried all their belongings with them in one or several bundles.

People stood crowded together in a line, holding

bowls waiting to be filled with what smelled to Shirley like minestrone. Some men and women, who had already received their meal, were seated at tables, eating.

It was the floor that captured Shirley's attention. She walked slowly back and forth across the room, looking at the people as they ate, then down at their feet.

Nothing.

She moved on to the food line, starting at the back and moving slowly forward, still peering intently at the floor.

Of course. There they were. The only pair of feet on the line without shoes—only stockings. And thin wool socks.

Shirley looked up to observe the rest of the person.

It was a woman. Not young, but with all she'd no doubt been through, you couldn't really tell, Shirley thought. She was thin; her hair was white and sparse. She was dressed in so many layers of rags, it was hard to tell where one layer ended and another began. Shirley sniffed the air around the woman, who paid no attention. But as she left the line with her full bowl, Shirley stopped her.

"Huh?" the woman grunted.

"Size nine, right?" Shirley asked.

"How many times do I have to tell you freaks! I'm an atheist!" the woman shrieked. No one looked up.

Shirley was unfazed. "The fire last night," she said calmly. "You were there, weren't you?"

A look of panic filled the woman's eyes. She dropped

her soup bowl and headed for a side door. Shirley ducked most of the soup splashes and took off after her. They were in an alley, a bad choice for the frightened woman. A wire fence blocked the way to the next street. The woman turned and faced Shirley.

Sighing, the woman gave up. "You cops," she said with a small chuckle. "You just keep gettin' younger 'n' younger."

"I'm not a cop," Shirley said softly. "I'm really not. And I'm not going to hurt you. I just want some information."

The woman eyed her curiously.

"You were at that fire last night," Shirley said. "Wasn't."

"I can smell the smoke in your clothes," Shirley told her. She let her backpack drop off her left shoulder and reached into it. "And I believe"—she pulled out the bag containing the old sneakers—"these are yours."

The woman's face lit up. "Thought I'd never see those again! And I'd just broken 'em in, too!" She reached for the bag, but Shirley pulled it away.

"Did you see anything last night?" Shirley asked. "At the fire?"

The woman looked at the shoes, then back at Shirley. "What's it worth to you?" she asked.

Shirley thought a minute, then reached into her backpack again.

"Tuna sandwich?" she asked, smiling. "And the shoes, of course."

"Hmmph," the woman snorted. "Tuna's never been my favorite."

"Whoever set that fire almost killed you," Shirley said. "Don't you want them caught?"

The woman hesitated, then held out her hands. Shirley passed the shoes and sandwich to the woman. The woman took a bite of the sandwich while Shirley waited patiently.

"I saw . . . nothing," the woman said.

Shirley waited.

"But I *heard* something. A terrible scream. Terrible. And it wasn't a woman! 'S all I know." She gave Shirley a nod, indicating that the conversation was finished, then took another bite of the sandwich.

CHAPTER

It was after dinner. Shirley was up in her attic room, peering intently through her microscope. "Burned fabric," she mumbled to herself. "And skin. Charred skin. . . ."

"Shirley, dear!" Gran was at the bottom of the stairs.

"What is it, Gran?"

"It's late."

"I know. I'm just about finished."

"I want you to come down here before you go to bed and try this new *chi quong* exercise!"

"Uh—"

"Come on, now. It's very relaxing. It'll help you sleep better."

Well, Shirley thought, *I guess I could use that.*

"Okay, Gran," she called. "Just let me put some things away and I'll be right down."

* * *

The next morning Shirley made sure she was on time for school. She even rode her bike to get there faster. But when she pulled up in front of the school gate, she saw a fire truck, policemen, and more CRIME SCENE tape. The tape surrounded what had been the gardener's shed, which was now completely gutted by fire. It was a burned-out shell, with curious students milling around it. Shirley put her bike in the steel stand and joined them.

In the middle of the group, Shirley saw Inspector Markie talking with Ms. Stratmann. The inspector was a tall, handsome African American with a neat mustache. He wore a suit and tie.

"Why would anyone do such a thing?" Ms. Stratmann was saying, shaking her head. "I just don't understand!"

Suddenly Inspector Markie turned. He had seen someone heading quickly toward the school building, and he made a beeline for him.

"Bo," Shirley whispered to herself. "He thinks Bo had something to do with this." She followed the students to the front door of the school, where Inspector Markie had cornered Bo.

"We meet again, Boris," Inspector Markie said. Ms. Stratmann was at his side.

"It's Bo," the boy answered, staring at his shoes.

"Let's go to my office," Ms. Stratmann said, pointing, and the three of them went into the school.

20

Without hesitation, Shirley walked to the side of the building. She knew exactly which of the first-floor windows belonged to the office of the headmistress.

Bo was scrunched in a chair in the middle of the room, his arms folded. Ms. Stratmann was seated behind her desk, and Inspector Markie was standing over Bo. Although hidden by a bush in front of the open window, Shirley had a clear view. She could see between the branches, but from inside, no one could see her.

"Okay, Bo," Inspector Markie began, "where were you last night?"

"Home," Bo answered, his head down.

"With your parents?"

"They were at bingo." Suddenly Bo looked up. "You don't think I did it?"

Inspector Markie shook his head in exasperation. "You know, you were *this close* to reform school. Everyone went through a lot of trouble to get you in here. And this is how you pay them back?"

Bo looked directly at the inspector. "I didn't do it," he said. "I *swear*!"

Ms. Stratmann and the inspector exchanged glances.

"You're not even checking on anyone else, right?" Bo asked defiantly. "You're so sure it's me!"

"Okay, why shouldn't we think it's you?" Inspector

Markie asked. "I have never been called to this school before today, and a fire is set one day after you start here."

"I didn't do it!" Bo insisted.

Ms. Stratmann leaned over her desk. "We took a big chance letting you in here, Mr. Sawchuk," she said through tight lips. "Until this investigation is over, I have no choice but to suspend you."

"Yeah, *great!*" Bo shouted, getting up from the chair and heading for the door. "Just *great!*" He slammed the door behind him.

During a break between classes, Shirley snuck outside. It wasn't hard getting into the shed from behind. A shell of wall blocked Shirley from view, and both policemen were guarding the front, grumbling about how long it was taking Forensics to arrive.

Shirley slipped the shower caps over her shoes, put on the latex gloves, and began to look around. There, on what remained of the door, she found a wad of gum.

Gum. Just like at the other fire.

Quickly she scraped it off the door with her knife and slipped it into a plastic bag.

Shirley reached into her backpack and took out a book. She flipped the cover open, revealing hollowed-out pages that held a tiny plastic bottle of talcum powder, two artist's brushes, and Scotch tape. She sprinkled some powder on the brass door handle and carefully brushed most of it away. Then she pressed the tape up against the remaining powder on the handle and lifted off a clear set of wavy lines.

"Oh, good, hey, it's about time," she heard one of the policemen say. *The forensics people must have arrived*, she thought. *Time to go!*

CHAPTER

After school Shirley rode her bicycle through town to the Sawchuk Fish Store and stepped inside the back entrance. She was in the room where the fish were cleaned and prepared for sale. Bo was scaling a bass, his head down and his mouth working hard on a piece of gum. He looked up and started at the sight of Shirley in the doorway.

"What are you doing here?" he asked sullenly, and went back to the bass.

"Would you mind rolling up your shirtsleeves?" Shirley asked.

Bo snorted. "Why should I?"

Shirley tapped her foot. "I don't have all day."

Bo looked at her as if she were nuts, but he rolled up both sleeves anyway.

"Okay. Now your pant legs."

Bo shook his head. "You're not just weird," he told

her, "you're sick." He bent down and rolled up his pant legs too.

Shirley nodded. "Right," she said, "it's what I thought."

"Yeah, and what's that?"

"You're not burned."

Bo sighed. "Right. I'm not burned. So?"

"So: You didn't torch the gardener's shed or that old building on Seventeenth."

"I know that," Bo said, and straightened his clothes.

Shirley put her backpack on a clean end of the table and opened it. She handed Bo the plastic bag with the piece of burned fabric.

Bo looked at her blankly.

"The Seventeenth Street fire! I found a witness who heard a scream. And I found this burnt piece of cloth!"

"Yeah?"

"Under a microscope, I saw charred flesh. And I also saw hair follicles!"

"Gross!" was Bo's response.

"Don't you get it?" Shirley took a deep breath and let it out. "That says that someone—probably the one who set the fire—was burned severely on an arm or a leg!"

"So what?" Bo replied. "That was another fire. They're blaming me for the gardener's shed at school." He put down the fish and turned to get a mop and bucket.

"Bo, it was the same arsonist," Shirley said. She

handed him two more plastic bags, each containing a wad of gum. "There was gum on the door handles at each site! Don't you see? It's like a signature!"

Bo began to mop the floor. "So, go to the police," he said.

"I would," Shirley said, "but we have a problem."

"*We?*" Bo asked.

"We," Shirley answered, nodding. "Your fingerprints are all over the place."

Bo dropped the mop. "Huh?"

"From when that guy pushed you into the shed."

Now she had Bo's attention. He chewed his gum harder.

"You see, based on the evidence so far," Shirley finished, "you seem to be the prime suspect."

Bo just stared at her.

"So." Shirley folded her arms. "Who's setting you up?"

Bo brushed his hands on his trousers and stormed out of the store.

Shirley followed him out, jumped on her bike, and pedaled after him. "Where are you going?" she called.

"Don't get involved!" Bo called back, and began to run faster.

"I know you didn't do it!" Shirley yelled.

Bo stopped for a second, but only a second. Again he picked up his pace.

"Who's the guy who jumped you?" Shirley asked. She had almost caught up with him.

Bo stopped and sighed. "I'm not gonna shake you, am I?"

"Nope."

"Look . . . if I tell you who the guy was, will you leave?"

Shirley didn't answer. "Why's he after you?" she asked, looking right into Bo's eyes.

Bo raised his hands in exasperation and then let them flop to his sides. "Because! He wants me to steal stuff from the kids at Sussex. His name's Sean."

Shirley nodded. "But why did he say you owed him?"

Bo turned away. "I did a dumb thing," he said quietly. "It was stupid, but you had to shoplift stuff to get into the gang." He turned back to her. "I got caught, okay? I was on my way to juvie, but my social worker saved my butt. Steve talked the judge into a probation, where if I go to the academy and check in with him every week, I don't have to go to juvie. And I have to quit the gang."

"Sounds like he's a good guy," Shirley said.

"Steve? Yeah, he's great. I was lucky to draw him. You should see some of the other social workers down there."

They were strolling together. Shirley walked her bike, holding its handlebars. "So what's the problem with Sean?" she asked.

Bo held out his hand, revealing his tattoo. "You can't just 'quit' a gang," he said.

"So Sean set you up for arson." Shirley's puzzle now had some of its missing pieces.

Now Bo's did too. "Look—I gotta go find Steve," he said, and began to run.

Shirley hopped on her bike and went after him again. "Hey! Wait up! You can't shake me!"

They were in one of the offices at the East Side Community Center. Behind a gray metal desk sat a dark, pleasant-looking man in his early thirties. He stood up as Bo and Shirley entered.

"Hey, buddy!" The man reached out to shake Bo's hand. Then he looked over at Shirley. "Who's your friend?" he asked.

"Her name's Shirley," Bo replied. "Shirley, this is, uh, Steve, he's my social worker. The one who— y'know—"

"Saved your butt," Shirley finished.

Steve laughed. "Nice to meet you, Shirley." He sat back down behind his desk. "So!" He gave them a wide grin. "What brings you here?"

When Bo was finished with his story, there was silence in the room. Shirley had paced while he'd talked, just listening.

Steve sat still, his elbows resting on his desk, his hands steepled under his chin.

"These are pretty serious charges," he said finally.

"You don't believe me?" Bo asked quickly.

"I always believe you, Bo," Steve answered. He thought for a moment. "Look," he said, "here's what I'll do. I'll talk to Sean—"

"You know Sean well?" Shirley interrupted.

"Sure. He and a few of these other guys are clients of mine." Steve turned back to Bo. "I'll see what I can do to keep him off your case. But about these fires, Bo, you make sure you're where you're supposed to be when you're supposed to be there and stay out of trouble! It's school, work, and home. Got it?"

"Yeah," Bo agreed.

"Because everything's on the line, here, right?"

Bo nodded. "Thanks, Steve," he said, standing up to leave.

"What for?" Steve asked.

"Ah, you know. Listening. Being my friend."

Steve smiled. "Any time, kid, any time. You know, I'm here whenever one of my kids needs me."

"Yeah, day or night . . . I know."

They shook hands over the desk. As Shirley followed Bo to the door, she stopped in front of a framed animation cel of a cartoon character. She tapped the silver frame with her finger and smiled at Steve.

"Cool cel," she said.

"Thanks." Steve smiled back.

They stood in the hall around the corner from Steve's office. Bo glanced at his watch.

"Hey, I gotta go back to work," he said.

Shirley raised her eyes toward a door with a brass plate reading LADIES. "I need to—um—use the facilities. You go ahead."

Bo grinned. "You sure I'll be okay on my own?"

"No-oo," Shirley told him.

He shook his head at her and laughed. He turned and rounded the corner.

But Shirley didn't move toward the rest room. She had spied Sean across the hall. Bo obviously hadn't noticed him. Shirley watched to see if Sean would head for Steve's office, and he did.

She heard Steve greet Sean as the office door closed behind him. She leaned back against the wall. She didn't have to be home until dinner, which she knew would be late. Her dad was giving a speech that evening at the embassy.

She removed a box of juice from her backpack and stuck its plastic straw through the hole at the top. Then she took the straw and tossed it in a trash container against the wall.

She had time. She would wait. Sean was a client of Steve's, and it was logical that he would visit this office. But his being there suited Shirley's purposes. It would save her the trouble of tracking him down.

Five minutes passed.

Ten.

Shirley hadn't heard a sound. No office doors opening or closing. No people, but it was after hours, and everyone had probably left for the day.

Except for Steve, who'd said he was always there when his clients needed him.

Finally: a creaking noise from around the corner.

Shirley took a deep breath and held up the juice box.

"Yeah," she heard a young voice say. "See ya."

The sound of a closing door. Footsteps came toward Shirley. She listened, counted the steps, clutched the juice container. She jumped forward . . .

. . . and collided with Sean. She squished the juice box against him, spilling the dark red liquid all over his shirt and open leather jacket. The gum he'd been chewing dropped out of his mouth.

"You *moron!*" he shouted. He pulled off his stained jacket. "Look what you—"

"Oh, I'm so sorry!" Shirley exclaimed, waving her arms, a dipstick expression on her face. "I'm *such* a klutz! My dad calls me a walking *tsunami*, which is like this giant *wave*, y'know? Whenever it hits, it destroys docks, buildings, even whole *villages!*" She looked at him with wide eyes. "Can you imagine what it would be like to actually *surf* a *tsunami*? Wouldn't it be *so* cool?"

Sean was busy with his leather jacket. He had pulled it off and was examining it, but Shirley was peering at the large bandage wrapped above his elbow. Scabbing showed around the edges.

"What kind of a nut *are* you!" Sean mumbled, trying to wipe the juice from his clothes.

Shirley pulled a tissue from her pocket and dabbed at the stains. "Here, just let me help you—"

Sean pulled back. "Just get away! Get lost, you idiot!"

Shirley gave him her best airhead look. "Hey, like o-kay," she said. She turned away from him and rolled her eyes as she left the building.

CHAPTER

Shirley spent the evening with Gran and her dad. She lay on the hearth rug with Watson after dinner and tried to concentrate on her homework while she thought about what the next day would bring.

Robert Holmes relaxed in his easy chair, attempting to finish the morning paper, which had even more holes clipped out of it.

"Someday," he asked dryly, "will I receive a paper *intact*, do you think?"

"Someday, maybe," Shirley answered with a grin.

"How's school going?" he asked. "You haven't said a word about it all evening."

"It's fine."

"Things all right with Ms. Stratmann?"

"As well as can be expected," Shirley replied. "How are things at the embassy?"

"Oh—as well as can be expected," he answered with a smile.

"How about that *chi quong* exercise I taught you last night?" Gran asked Shirley. "It helped ease tension, didn't it?"

Shirley rolled over on her side and propped her head up with a hand. "It did," she said. "Didn't I tell you this morning how well I slept?"

"Mm-hmm. Just reminding you. How about trying it now? If you're finished with that homework, of course."

"Sure."

They stood together in the middle of the room, backs straight, hands at their sides, knees slightly bent.

"Tongue to the roof of the mouth," Gran reminded her. "Breathe from the diaphragm."

"Uh-huh."

"Now," Gran said, "bow."

They bowed.

"Squat," Gran instructed. "Place your hands over your feet. Exhale—"

"I remember," Shirley said.

"Now, inhale deeply; straighten your legs, keeping your palms flat against them as you rise. Keep those legs straight, dear, that's the good stretching part."

They repeated the exercise quietly several times.

"There, now," Gran said. "How does that feel?"

"Relaxing," Shirley admitted. "It does. How about you, Dad? Join us?"

"Maybe on the day I receive a paper intact," he replied.

* * *

The next school day ended without incident for Shirley. She got her bike from the stand and was about to pedal away when Bo ran up to her.

"Hey, Shirley!" he said.

"Hey, Bo."

He looked away from her bashfully, kicking a foot at the gravel. "Look, I just wanted to—uh— You know, because of everything . . . you know . . ."

"You're welcome," Shirley said. She noticed that he was dressed in his work clothes—jeans and a plaid flannel shirt. "Are you still suspended?"

Bo shrugged. "Steve called Stratmann. She didn't lift the suspension, but he said she didn't sound so ticked off, like before, y'know? So maybe I'll get to come back soon, huh?"

Shirley raised her eyebrows. "Maybe not."

"What do you mean?" Bo asked.

Shirley got off her bike and gave Bo a serious look. "I met your friend, Sean, yesterday afternoon. His left arm is badly burned. He's the arsonist."

Bo shook his head, worried. "Look, Shirley, don't mess with Sean, okay?"

"We know he torched the shed to set you up," Shirley explained. She knew she was only going to get into trouble with Bo.

Bo sighed. Shirley Holmes was the *stubbornest* person he'd ever met!

"But why the Seventeenth Street building?" Shirley asked him.

Bo ambled away, down the dirt path. Shirley caught up, walking her bike. She studied him as she waited for an answer.

Bo gave in. "Guys like Sean don't do stuff like that for kicks," he said.

"For money?" Shirley asked, and then she figured it out.

"*Ohh! Sure!* An insurance scam!" she exclaimed. "The owner has the building torched to collect the cash!"

"It's heavy," Bo said. "Told ya."

Shirley leaned on her bike. "What we have to do is find out who owns that building," she said.

"No way!" Bo said, alarmed. "Stay out of it! I mean it, Shirley!"

Shirley sat on her bike seat and put her feet on the pedals.

As she pedaled away, Bo yelled, "Hey, look, Steve's right. My butt's really on the line and . . ."

Shirley kept pedaling slowly. "Do you have a choice here?" she asked without looking back.

Bo was running after her now. "I—"

"Just come with me," Shirley said. "Come on, run! Are you out of shape or what?"

Bo slapped his hand against his head but hurried to keep up.

CHAPTER

"This is your *house?*" Bo breathed as they approached the circular drive.

"Uh-huh."

"It's—it's a castle!"

"It's not a castle. It's a big old Victorian," Shirley said.

"It's big, all right. How many people live here?"

"Me, my dad, my grandmother, and Watson."

"Who's Watson, your butler?"

Shirley laughed. "You'll meet him," she said.

Gran was doing Tai Chi when Shirley knocked on her apartment door.

"Come in!" was the cheery answer. Gran didn't like to stop in the middle of an exercise.

"Hi, Gran. Meet Bo!"

"Hello, Bo," Gran said on an exhale, bending deeply from the waist.

Bo didn't answer. He was staring around the sitting room. He gaped at the furnishings, paintings, sculptures, death masks, spears, and other artifacts from Gran's travels around the world.

Shirley elbowed him in the ribs. "Gran said hello," she prompted. "Where're your manners?"

"Uh—oh, sorry," Bo stammered. "Uh—hello."

Gran began to move her arms in great waves, the palms of her hands facing each other.

Bo looked at Shirley for an explanation but didn't get one. Instead Shirley moved to the bookcase and pushed the little button on the shelf. The bookcase revolved.

"Whoa!" Bo said as the staircase was revealed. "Cool," he murmured, but Shirley was already halfway up, and he followed quickly.

Shirley slung her backpack to the floor and went straight to her computer. Bo had no interest in the computer; the room was what fascinated him. Suddenly his eyes took in the portrait on the wall above the overstuffed chair. He moved toward it and stared hard.

"Who's the guy in the weird hat?" he asked. "He looks kind of like—"

"Sherlock Holmes," Shirley finished. Her eyes didn't leave the screen.

"Sherlock Holmes, huh? Hey, your name's Holmes, right? Is he some kind of relative?"

"Great-granduncle," Shirley said, tapping the keyboard.

"The name sounds familiar," Bo said. "Where've I heard it?"

Now Shirley stopped and turned to face him. "You don't know *Sherlock Holmes?*" she asked, stunned.

"Oh, hey! Yeah! Yeah, wasn't he a real famous detective about a gazillion years ago?"

Shirley rolled her eyes and turned back to her computer. "Right," she said. "A *gazillion* years."

"No, really, there are a lot of books by him, aren't there?"

"Books *about* him, yes. Many," Shirley replied.

"Sure, sure," Bo said, almost to himself. "A really famous guy!"

"Right."

"I didn't make the connection! No *wonder* you're such a snoop!"

Shirley made no comment but went on working. Bo continued to examine the room. On a small table stood a framed photograph of a beautiful woman. He picked it up.

"Who's this?" he asked.

Shirley didn't look up. "My mom," she said softly.

"Oh. She around?"

"No."

Bo waited for her to explain. Shirley typed.

"So? Where is she?" Bo asked.

"She's away. Come here!"

"What?" He went to look over her shoulder.

"Look!" Shirley pointed to the screen. "The owner! Of the warehouse!"

Bo looked at the highlighted name: Goldfar.

"Goldfar," he said.

"Go downstairs awhile," Shirley said impatiently. "I need to find some more stuff. I'll be down in a minute."

Bo shrugged and made his way down the stairs. Gran was still doing Tai Chi, and he didn't want any part of it. He continued downstairs and found his way to the kitchen.

Shirley's father had arrived home and was emptying papers from his briefcase, piling them on a countertop. He smiled at Bo.

"Hello there," he said.

"Hi," Bo managed to answer.

"You're a classmate of Shirley's?" Mr. Holmes asked.

"Uh—right. Bo Sawchuk."

"Robert Holmes." Mr. Holmes stuck out his hand, and Bo shook it awkwardly, murmuring "Gladda-meetcha."

"And—where is my daughter?"

"She's—um—upstairs. She'll be down in a minute."

"Mm-hmm," Mr. Holmes muttered, and began to shuffle through his paperwork.

At a loss for more conversation, Bo began to examine the kitchen. *So this is how the other half lives!* he thought. *They may be rich, but this family sure is weird!*

The refrigerator door seemed to be covered with family photos. Bo studied them, recognizing one.

"Your wife, huh?" he asked, pointing to it. Then he clumsily shoved his hands into his pockets. "I, uh, I mean I saw her picture upstairs."

Shirley's father continued to pore over his papers.

"So, um, when's she coming back?" Bo asked.

Mr. Holmes looked up. He blinked at Bo, then turned back to his papers. "My wife died three years ago," he said stiffly.

Bo's face reddened. But before he could apologize, Shirley appeared in the doorway. She had changed into jeans, a T-shirt, and a denim jacket. Her backpack was slung over her shoulder. She had pulled her hair back into two little-girlish pigtails, with barrettes holding each. She went to a canister on the counter and grabbed a chocolate bar from it.

"Hi, Dad," she said, pocketing the candy bar. She gave him a kiss on the cheek. "Ready?" she asked Bo.

"Ready for what?" he asked, but she was heading for the front door.

"I'm always following you!" he complained. He hurried after her.

"No, sometimes I've followed you," she reminded him. "Remember?"

"Yeah. Can't shake you."

"Right."

As they reached the door, they heard a loud sneeze. Both turned.

The basset hound was in his place on the hearth rug. He stared back at them and yawned.

"Oh," Shirley said, and laughed. "Meet Watson!"

Bo grinned. "Oh, so *that*'s . . ." But Shirley was already out the door.

CHAPTER  9

The name imprinted on the glass was Guy Jennings.

"It doesn't say anything about Goldfar," Bo whispered to Shirley.

"But this is the address I found, and it says Goldfar on the mailbox downstairs. Besides," she said, gesturing, "every other door has a company name except this one. This *must* be it. I'm sure they want to keep a low profile."

"Should we knock?"

Shirley shook her head. "Let's just go in. And play along with me."

She turned the knob quietly. "Not locked," she whispered, and opened the door.

They found themselves in a small anteroom containing an empty desk and some filing cabinets. Another door, behind the desk, stood open, and they could see a man with his back to them on the telephone. *"Forget it!"* the man yelled, and banged his fist on the arm of his chair. He was so angry, he didn't even hear Bo and Shirley as they entered.

"*You got your money!*" he bellowed into the phone, then listened a moment. Then: "So there were complications! That's *tough*!" Suddenly he whirled around in his chair and saw the two young people.

"Hi!" Shirley chirped. She looked at the nameplate on his desk. It too read GUY JENNINGS. "Are you Mr. Jennings?"

The man slammed down the phone.

"How did you two kids get in here? Whatta you want?"

Shirley pulled the chocolate bar out of her pack. "We're raising money for new floor hockey equipment!"

"Get outta here!"

Bo glanced quickly at Shirley, who was still smiling, her pigtails bouncing each time she moved her head. He jumped right in. "That's right, sir," he said politely. "It's a great cause. It keeps kids off the street. And you know what happens when good things keep kids off the street, right? Petty crime drops right off! Is that your Porsche parked out front, sir?"

Shirley bit her lower lip to keep from grinning.

Jennings stood up. "Okay, okay. Just a second." He pressed a buzzer on his desk, but no one answered it. "My secretary out there?" he mumbled. "Stella! *Stella!*" He shook his head. "Hang on a minute, I'll go get some petty cash." He strode past them and out the door.

Without a moment of hesitation, Shirley reached across Jennings's desk and grabbed the phone receiver, immediately pushing the Redial button. Then she pressed Speaker.

They both heard the phone ring once before it was picked up.

"East Side Community Center. Steve Ryan speaking. How can I help you?"

Shirley hung up. Bo gasped.

Shirley looked at him. "Bo, get out there and intercept Mr. Jennings. I don't care what you have to do. I need to find something."

Bo nodded and went out into the anteroom. Shirley could hear him chattering as she went through the desk drawers. She had to be quick. There was no time, no time.

She found many papers but only one file folder in the bottom drawer. She didn't have to go through it; the file's tab showed her what she needed to know. She stuffed the folder into her backpack and calmed herself down, using the breathing techniques Gran had taught her.

When Jennings burst into the room again, followed by a worried Bo, Shirley was standing with her arms folded, looking bored.

"Well, gosh, what took you so long?" she asked.

Shirley yanked off her silly barrettes as she and Bo hurried down the steps of the office building.

"There's gotta be a mistake," Bo hissed at her.

"I don't think so," Shirley said. "Steve is involved in this, Bo. You know that animation cel he has framed in his office?"

"Yeah."

They were dashing down the steps, both panting.

"Wait'll we get outside," Shirley said.

They reached the office door and hurried out.

"Okay, we're outside," Bo said, and leaned against the iron railing. "What about the cel?"

"It's a signed original." She saw Bo's expression. "The artist signed it himself!" she explained.

"So?"

Shirley sighed. "*So*, Steve's a social worker! Do you know what those things cost? He couldn't afford to buy something like that on his salary!"

Bo got the picture, but he didn't want to believe it. "Look," he said, "maybe it was a gift. Y'know, from someone he helped who did okay in life. He'd never do this, Shirley."

Shirley touched his arm. "Bo, I know this is hard—"

Bo jerked his arm away. "He just wouldn't, that's all."

But Shirley was out of patience. "What we have to do is tail him. That's the only way we'll get any evidence!"

"No!" Bo cried angrily. "*We* don't have to do anything!" He charged down the steps and took off. Shirley's eyes followed him. She could guess where he was going.

It wasn't quite dusk when Shirley reached the community center. There was no sign of Bo, but she did catch sight of Steve as he came down the front steps.

Nice trench coat, Shirley thought. She followed him as he made his way down the street, and she watched him turn a corner, which she knew led to an alley. She took a breath and slowed down. She had time.

Aluminum trash cans and huge black bags of garbage stood at the entrance to the alley. Shirley ducked behind them and took out her tiny camera.

She saw Steve, Sean, and another boy. Steve reached into his coat pocket and took out an envelope, which he handed to Sean. Sean picked through its contents, counting money.

Snap! went the shutter on Shirley's camera.

"The rest when it's done," Steve said.

"Yeah, yeah," Sean muttered.

"The place is just for storage, it's deserted, but you make sure no one's there before *anything* goes down, understand?" Steve asked, waving his forefinger in Sean's face.

Sean slapped Steve's hand away. "Whaddya think I am, stupid? Like this is the first time?"

"It'll be cool," the other boy said. "No problem."

Shirley jammed herself farther behind the trash as the three left the alley. Steve went in one direction, Sean and his friend in the other.

Shirley took a sniff of the trash. *Boy, I'm really gonna need a shower later,* she thought. She followed Steve back toward the community center, where she saw Bo waiting next to Steve's car. He looked confused and angry. He tapped his knuckles against the car's hood as he waited. Steve's arrival from the street rather than the center surprised him.

Shirley turned her back, pretending to be interested in a hardware store window display. She was in plain sight, but neither Bo nor Steve took any notice of her.

"You weren't in your office!" Bo growled. "But your car's still here!"

Steve raised his eyebrows and smiled. "Is that a crime?" he asked jovially.

"*That* isn't," Bo said.

Steve's smile disappeared. "What's up, Bo?" he asked.

Bo stared him down. "I keep remembering things, okay? Like last year when an old strip mall got torched. Sean got a new leather jacket. And you put up that cartoon in your office."

"I don't follow you," Steve said. He took his keys out of his pocket and began to move toward the driver's side of his car.

Bo blocked his path. "Anxious to get away, huh, Steve?" Bo looked as if he wanted to cry. Everything about Steve's body language gave him away. "I didn't want to believe it," Bo said. "But now I know it's true. You get paid to burn down buildings! The insurance comes through, and everybody makes out! Only Sean does the actual torching for a measly cut of what *you* get!"

"Hey, Bo." Steve held up his hands, palms out. "You *know* me."

"Do me a favor," Bo said. "Tell me if I'm right."

Steve leaned heavily against his car. "Okay, look: So I don't play strictly by the book. That's what makes me good at what I do."

"How do you figure that?" Bo asked with a sneer.

Steve gave him a pleading look. "Don't you see? I help each kid according to his needs. Guys like Sean— there's no way they'd ever have the potential you do. You can cut it in a good school. You have smarts. You can even get a scholarship if you stay cool. But Sean, Jason, those guys— Hey, I get them well-paying work."

"That's sick logic, man," Bo said softly.

"Was it sick when I kept you out of Juvenile Hall?"

"That was by the book!"

Steve shook his head. "No. You're a decent kid, Bo, but nobody cared about that. That judge owed me a favor. I called it in." Steve pulled open the door of his car and got in, edging Bo out of the way. With a roar, the car pulled away from the curb.

A stunned Bo stared after it. Shirley came up beside him.

"Hi," she said.

"I should have known you'd be here," Bo sighed. "Did you hear?"

"Yes. I'm sorry."

"Yeah. Me too."

"But we're not through yet," Shirley said. "Come on, walk with me!" She began to move briskly down the street, back toward the alley where Steve had met Sean.

"Where're we going?" Bo asked, keeping up.

"There's going to be another fire tonight. In a few minutes it'll be dark, and that's when they'll do it."

"How do you—"

"Jennings had a list of Goldfar buildings in one of his files. That's just one of his names, but most of the Goldfar places are within blocks of each other. There are two more—another on Seventeenth and a warehouse on Marshall Street."

"Yeah?"

"They're going to torch the one on Marshall."

"How do you know?" Bo was panting now.

"There were dates next to each address. The Marshall Street warehouse is tonight. Hurry up, Bo! Boy, you should really start working out!"

CHAPTER  10

The warehouse was deserted. It was dark, but there was no sign of Sean, the other boy, or anyone else. One streetlamp glowed dimly on the corner. A man in rags shuffled by, pushing his belongings in a supermarket cart.

"What now?" Bo asked. "They're not here."

"It's dark, but it's still early. We'll wait," Shirley told him. "Come on."

They walked around to the side of the building.

"Stop," Shirley said, and held out her arm. "I can get through this window. You wait here and go for help if anything happens." She cleared shards of glass from the broken windowpane.

"No way!" Bo whispered. "You're not going in there by yourself!"

"I have to!" She hoisted herself up to the ledge. "I want pictures of them when they get here. We're dead meat if they catch us both!"

Bo gritted his teeth. There was no arguing with Shirley when she had her mind made up.

"I'm in!" Shirley whispered from inside. "There's a closet or something here. I'm going into it! You watch!"

Bo took a breath and inched over to the corner of the building, pressing his back against the wall. He peeked out at the street.

Nothing.

He could hear his heart beating. He backed up against the side of the warehouse. Everything was so quiet, he knew he could hear anyone approaching. Sean . . . and probably Jason, Bo figured. They always hung out together, more than with any of the other guys in the gang. Would there be anyone else? What was Shirley doing in the closet? he wondered. Probably setting up all that high-tech stuff she kept in her backpack.

He crept over to the window. "Shirley!" he whispered.

No answer. She probably couldn't hear him.

Suddenly there was a sharp noise, followed by the sound of glass breaking. Bo slammed himself back against the wall. The dim light from the streetlamp was gone. It was very dark now. Bo heard Sean's voice:

"Okay . . . no one's around. Anyone who'd've heard that lamp breakin' woulda made a move by now."

"Yeah, so let's do it, okay? You go ahead. Like we planned."

That was Jason, Bo knew. Sounded like just the two of them. What now? Bo couldn't warn Shirley. Should he go inside? Through the window or through the front? And maybe there were more guys, who knew?

Shirley had heard the glass breaking and figured out what it was. Her camera was ready. She peered out from behind the door and began snapping photos. Sean was in the main room. He didn't even glance her way. He was busy pouring gasoline on the floor and against the walls. Then he moved out of sight, and she could hear another door being opened. She heard the sloshing sounds of gas being poured in a different room.

Shirley held her breath. *I've got enough*, she thought. *I'll get back out through the window*. She carefully pushed the door a little wider and—

Standing right in front of her closet door was the other boy. Sean's friend. She hadn't heard him at all.

The boy grabbed Shirley and yanked the camera from her hand. "Hey, Sean!" the boy yelled.

"Shut up, Jason!" was the reply from deeper inside the warehouse.

"But you gotta see what I found!"

Sean appeared at the far end of the main room. His eyes widened at the sight of Jason holding Shirley by her arms. Shirley struggled to get away, but Jason was holding her too tightly.

"Well, well," Sean said, smiling and leaning into Shirley's face. He was chewing a thick wad of gum. "The walking tsunami!"

He yanked Shirley away from Jason and dragged her toward the room in which he'd just been pouring gasoline. "Come on," Sean said to Jason. "Let's finish up with the gas and get moving." Sean pushed Shirley into the room and locked the door behind him with a sliding latch.

Shirley could hear them on the other side of the door. She still had her backpack, and she rummaged through it for her Swiss Army knife. Frantically she began to work on the sliding lock.

"There's enough gas," Shirley heard Jason say. "Just get the matches lit and toss 'em!"

Uh-oh, Shirley thought.

"Yeah. Okay. You get to the door," Sean told Jason.

Shirley heard a door open. "Look who's here," she heard Jason say.

"I called the cops!" Shirley recognized the voice: Bo!

"Usually the cops call you," Sean said. "Hold him!"

Shirley heard scuffling outside the door. Was Bo all right? The doors were old, nearly rotted plywood, but not soft enough for Shirley to break out. She continued to work on the sliding lock with her knife, but was flung back as the door opened and Bo was thrown in on top of her.

"Bo!" she yelled. "Try not to let the door—"

It slammed shut.

"Close," she finished lamely.

Shirley and Bo crouched beside the door. Shirley had resumed working on the lock with her knife. Her expression was intense. She was totally focused.

"They teach you this at the academy?" Bo asked.

Suddenly there was a *whoosh* from the other room.

"They did it!" Bo cried, standing up. "They ignited it—"

"No way they're turning us into Crispy Critters," Shirley said calmly.

Bo watched her try to pick the lock. "Aw, that's not gonna work," he said, but at that moment they heard a *click*. It was the metal bar of the lock sliding back.

Shirley looked at Bo with a raised eyebrow and a smile.

In a split second they were through the door. Flames licked up the walls of the big main room and nearly covered the floor.

"The window!" Shirley said. "The one I came through—"

"Can't! There's fire blocking it!"

Frantically they looked around. Shirley ran into another room.

"In here!" she yelled, and Bo raced in. "This is a window! It faces the side street, but it's boarded up! Help me." She threw her shoulder against the boards desperately, and Bo began to pound on them.

"It's one floor up! What'll we do, jump?" he cried.

She kept striking the boards with her body. "Let's—worry—about that—after we get—these boards—*off*!" The rotted wood finally snapped. Smoke flooded the room as the air blew in through the empty window frame.

"Not a minute too soon!" Shirley grinned at Bo, then looked out the window. "And guess what we have *here*!"

"Fire escape!" Bo yelled, and barked a laugh. "Let's go!"

He hurried out the window and down the fire escape with Shirley right behind. Suddenly she felt herself jerked back. A nail!

"Bo! I'm stuck! My shirt caught on a nail—or something." She pulled and yanked, but it wouldn't give. Bo took the steps two at a time. He grabbed Shirley by the shoulders and wrenched her free, tearing her shirt. They took off down the fire escape and made it to the ground.

"Run!" Shirley screamed. They hit the sidewalk as the fiery warehouse exploded behind them. The force of the blast threw them into a scraggly island of weeds.

They raised their heads; they could hear the sirens of approaching fire trucks.

CHAPTER  11

Shirley and Bo stayed until the work was done.

Both of them were covered with soot. Their clothes were torn, and they had cuts and scratches on their arms and legs.

"What did your father say when you called?" Bo asked. They watched as the firefighters packed up their equipment.

"I got Gran. I said we were watching a fire being put out." Shirley looked down at her clothes and smiled at Bo.

He snorted a laugh. "Yeah, I guess she'll believe that, all right."

"Won't your folks wonder where *you* are?" Shirley asked.

"Uh-uh. Bingo."

Shirley wiped her hands on her jeans. "Guess they must really like bingo," she said.

"Yeah." Bo tightened his lips and nodded.

"Look, Bo." Shirley shoved her hands into her pockets and glanced away. "When I got caught up there . . . on the fire escape . . . I, uh, just wanted to say . . ."

"You're welcome," Bo said.

She nodded.

Both of them felt awkward. It was one thing to solve a crime and another to actually talk to each other.

Bo decided to go for it. "Shirley," he said, "can I ask you something?"

"Mmmmm?"

"About your mom . . ."

Shirley looked away. But as she did, she spotted Inspector Markie making his way toward them. "Look who's here," she said, nudging Bo.

The inspector looked tired. He was wiping his brow with a large handkerchief as he approached. He took a moment to examine the disheveled boy and gave a small chuckle.

"You okay, Boris?" he asked.

"Yeah . . . and it's Bo." Bo scowled.

"I want to thank you for calling," the inspector said. "We picked up your social worker and those punks. Seems your story holds up."

"I told you," Bo said.

"You have to know I'll still be keeping an eye on you," the inspector warned.

"You're welcome," Bo said. "You should thank my friend, too."

"What friend?"

58

Bo turned. Shirley was gone.

"Young man, I'd say you need a good night's sleep," Inspector Markie said. He punched Bo lightly on the shoulder and walked away.

Bo stood. *Shirley Holmes,* he said to himself, *you're the biggest mystery of all!*

Shirley managed to shower, wash her hair, and get into her nightshirt without being seen by Gran or Dad. Gran was asleep, and Dad was still at the embassy. There was just a faint whiff of smoke in Shirley's room, but that was all it was—a whiff. It would be gone by morning.

Shirley yawned. There was still something she had to do before bed.

She sat down at her desk and pulled a journal out of a drawer. She picked up a pen, dated a clean page, and began to write.

And so the perpetrators were all caught, she wrote at the end of the page. *Now Bo can get back to more important things, like learning how to deal with Ms. Stratmann. You'd like Bo, Mom. He's willing to fight for what he believes. Like you.*

She closed the book, put it back in the drawer, and stood up, ready at last for sleep.

"Oh," she said, "just one more thing." She faced her window, took a deep breath, and began to wave her arms slowly in the new *chi quong* exercise.

THE CASE OF THE RUBY RING

CHAPTER

A large hand-painted banner proclaiming ELECTION WEEK was strung across the top of the auditorium's stage.

The students filed into the room. Shirley Holmes and Bo Sawchuk were among the first to enter from the hall.

The students were neatly dressed. The boys wore white shirts with striped ties, gray slacks, and dark green blazers with the Sussex Academy crest on the pockets; the girls wore the same shirts, ties, and blazers, but instead of gray slacks, they wore plaid skirts and dark knee-high socks.

"Let's sit in the back," Bo suggested.

"No, let's move toward the front," Shirley said.

"Why?" Bo asked. "This is boring. Nothing but speeches. If I fall asleep, I don't want Stratmann to see me."

And indeed, there was Ms. Stratmann, the headmistress, staring out at her captive audience from center stage.

"It's *not* boring," Shirley said. She sat, pulling Bo down next to her by his sleeve. "Besides, there's more than speeches. Look at that!" She pointed to a pedestal near the microphone. Atop the pedestal was a large glass display case housing a dark blue velvet cushion.

Bo grunted. "What's that?" he asked.

"Look on the cushion," Shirley urged him. "Can you tell what it is?"

Bo squinted and peered. "Looks like jewelry."

"Looks like a magnificent ring!" Shirley told him. "That stone? It's a ruby!"

"Is it real?"

Shirley eyed a security guard near the stage-right curtain and nodded. "It's real, all right. See the red light? That glass is wired with an alarm. I know about that ring. It's famous. A picture of it's in our history book."

Bo shrugged. Fancy jewelry was not high on his list of things to think about.

He was on probation at Sussex Academy. He wasn't among the youngsters of the elite, whose parents could afford the academy's tuition. He'd once been in a gang, but fortunately the court had been lenient, seeing his potential. Shirley had seen it too, and had become his friend.

"Anyway," Shirley told him, "it's important whom we elect president of the student council. You should pay attention."

"Why?"

"So you know whom to vote for! For the whole year, that person will be speaking for you! The council president is the students' voice."

"Speaking for me, huh?" Bo curled his lip. "I don't like anyone speaking for me except *me.*"

"Mmmm, you've tried that, remember?" Shirley smiled.

Ms. Stratmann was tapping the microphone with a long fingernail.

"Can you all hear me?" she asked. She adjusted the mike, and it crackled and squealed. "Good." She gestured toward the display case. "Eight hundred years ago, King John wore the ring you see before you at the signing of the Magna Carta. Today we are privileged to have this symbol of democracy on loan to Sussex Academy so that all of you may view it and appreciate the principles it embodies."

There was a soft "ooohhh" from the audience.

"This loan was made possible by the parents of a new member of our student body." Ms. Stratmann nodded toward one of the students seated behind her. "Molly Hardy!"

A tall blond girl rose from her seat on the stage and smiled. The students applauded loudly. Molly sat down again.

"Did Stratmann get this excited when I first came to Sussex?" Bo joked. Shirley elbowed him.

As the applause faded, Ms. Stratmann continued.

"Sussex Academy is the first to display this ring publicly in over a hundred years," she announced proudly. "And Molly, herself a vice presidential candidate, asked her parents to loan us this ring in honor of our own democratic process: the election of the Sussex student council!"

After a moment of reverential silence, Ms. Stratmann went on. "And now, we'll hear what our presidential candidates have to say to us today. . . ."

"Look at that guy," Bo sneered. He jerked his chin toward one of the candidates sitting on the stage behind Ms. Stratmann. "He knows he's gonna win. He thinks he's God's gift to the world!"

Shirley eyed the boy. His real name was Stirling. Stirling Patterson. But everyone called him Stink.

"He's just cocky," Shirley whispered. "His father owns a chain of joke shops."

Ms. Stratmann pressed her palms together. "First we'll hear from our presidential candidates, Alicia Gianelli and Stirling Patterson!"

There were cheers from the audience and cries of *"Stink! Stink!"* from the boy's fan club in the back. Bo clapped unenthusiastically as both students stood up.

Stink bowed gracefully toward Alicia, his left arm sweeping low to the ground. "Ladies first!" he announced.

"Oh, *please*," Bo whispered. Shirley smiled.

Alicia Gianelli walked hesitantly toward the microphone. She was small for her age, but she had dark eyes that seemed to flash when she was excited.

The auditorium was not large. Sussex Academy prided itself on the small size of its classes. Its admissions committee turned away hundreds of applicants each year. But still, there were those long rows of wooden pews, and the entire student body staring at Alicia. *No*, she told herself. *You can't be nervous about one speech!* She cleared her throat. As she prepared to speak, a brownish liquid began to seep from under the curtain toward her feet. Alicia didn't notice. "Teachers," she began, "fellow students and—"

"Can't hear you!" someone yelled from the audience.

"Speak up!"

"Louder!"

Alicia lost her focus. She glanced over at her running mate, Molly, who nodded encouragingly. Alicia nodded back and straightened her shoulders. "Teachers . . . fellow students . . . Ms. Stratmann: If elected, I promise to—"

"Fix the mike!" a boy cried. Some students laughed.

That was the problem, Alicia realized. The mike was too high. She reached out and grabbed the metal stand. Suddenly her expression froze.

"What's with her?" Bo whispered to Shirley. "Bad case of stage fright?"

"Her eyes—" Shirley began.

All at once Alicia's body began to vibrate. Sparks flew from the microphone stand. Alicia moaned, her eyes grew wider, and her body shook.

In a flash Molly Hardy was out of her chair. She rushed toward Alicia, her book bag in her hands. It happened so quickly that later no one could quite remember the order of things. One moment Alicia Gianelli was clutching the electrified microphone while the audience of students and teachers sat horrified and stunned; the next, Molly had thrown her book bag over the frightened girl's hands and pulled her to the floor.

Alicia collapsed into Molly's arms.

"Alicia!" Molly cried into the girl's ear. "Alicia! It's all right, you're all right."

Ms. Stratmann hurried over. "Can you hear me, Alicia?" she asked, bending over the two girls.

"Uh-huh," Alicia managed to answer. She looked up. "Molly," she whispered weakly, "you saved my life."

"Yes, well done, Molly!" Ms. Stratmann said. "Very quick thinking! That book bag you used—"

"It's rubber," Molly explained. "It interrupted the circuit. It was the only thing I could think of."

"You saved my life," Alicia repeated.

A crowd had gathered around the stage. Instead of hovering over Alicia with everyone else, Shirley walked to the microphone. Bo was at her side.

"What are you looking at?" Bo asked. "What's that stuff on the ground?"

"The grounding wire to the mike's been cut," Shirley said.

"Yeah?" Bo asked.

Shirley knelt and touched the brown liquid on the floor with her finger. She sniffed it. Following the trail of the puddle, she saw that it had come from behind the curtain.

"So, what is it?" Bo asked.

"Root beer," Shirley answered.

"Huh?"

She motioned to Bo to follow, and together they slipped behind the closed curtain. They could hear the voices on the other side. Alicia was apparently trying to stand up.

"Are you sure you can walk?" Ms. Stratmann was asking.

"I . . . I think so . . ."

"Molly, would you please take Alicia to the infirmary?" There were sounds of shuffling and footsteps.

"C'mon," Shirley said to Bo. They crept behind a piece of scenery left over from the school's fall musical. "Look." She indicated an empty can on the floor.

"Root beer," Bo acknowledged.

From her blazer pocket, Shirley extracted a small plastic bag and a pencil. She used the pencil to lift the can and place it in the bag.

"Check *that* out," Bo said. He pointed to a discarded STINK FOR PRESIDENT flyer on the floor.

"Mmm, but look what's *on* it," Shirley said.

"Some kind of tread marks?" Bo asked.

"Yeah . . . but they're so small," Shirley said. "And made from the root beer. Someone must have stepped in it. She picked up the flyer, and it went into her backpack with the bagged soda can.

CHAPTER  2

In the infirmary on the first floor, Alicia lay on a cot. The nurse had left her to rest, with Molly for company. Everything in the room was white and gray: walls, floor, ceiling, privacy curtain. There was a print on one wall of a Norman Rockwell painting: a child in a doctor's office.

Alicia's head was turned to the side, and Molly was thumbing through a textbook.

Shirley entered softly. "Sleeping?" she mouthed to Molly. They both looked at Alicia. She opened her eyes.

"Hi, Shirley. Thanks for coming." Alicia propped herself up.

"How are you feeling?" Shirley asked.

"Better, thanks."

"Listen, Alicia, can I borrow your shoe?" Shirley asked.

Alicia didn't ask why. Shirley often made weird requests. Alicia pushed her legs forward on the cot. Shirley pulled off one brown oxford and sniffed its sole.

Molly wrinkled her nose and raised an eyebrow at Alicia.

Alicia smiled. "Molly, this is Shirley Holmes. Shirley, meet Molly Hardy, my new best friend. First she agrees to be my running mate at the very last minute, and then—*then* she saves my life!"

Molly dropped her eyes. "Come on," she said softly.

"It was an impressive rescue," Shirley told her. She picked up Alicia's foot and put her shoe back on.

Molly was shaking her head. "It was a reflex, really. I just knew I had to get her hands off that metal stand."

"Is it okay if I sit?" Shirley asked, and Molly jumped up to pull over another chair.

"Thanks." Shirley looked down at the small girl on the cot. "I'm really glad you're okay, Alicia."

"It was scary."

"I know. But—there's something you ought to know." Shirley's face was serious.

"What?" Alicia frowned.

"This wasn't an accident," Shirley said.

"*What?*" Molly cried. The book dropped from her lap.

Shirley continued to speak to Alicia. "Somebody arranged for you to be standing in a pool of liquid. It was root beer. And somebody cut the mike's ground wire. So you were a perfect conductor for the electricity."

"Come on! You're kidding me, right?" Molly asked.

Alicia knew better. She made a wry face at Molly. "Welcome to Sussex Academy, Molly," she said dryly. "And to Stink's stupid jokes!"

"Stink!" Molly looked from Alicia to Shirley.

Alicia sighed. "It's exactly like something he would do. And root beer is his favorite drink!"

"Hey! *Hey!*"

Someone was yelling in the hall. A man.

Shirley rose quickly and left the room, just in time to see the security guard running toward the headmistress's office. "Ms. Stratmann!" he was shouting. He was coughing at the same time, holding a large white handkerchief to his mouth. *"Ms. Stratmann!"*

Shirley grabbed up her backpack and followed him as he burst into the office. He gasped, trying to catch his breath. Mrs. Fish, the headmistress's secretary, got to her feet and *harrumph*ed. "Excuse *me*," she said, peering over her bifocals. Shirley stood in the office doorway.

"Call the police!" the security guard wheezed. "Ms. Stratmann! *Call the police!*"

"Whew!" Mrs. Fish waved away the air as she approached the guard. "What is that smell?"

Ms. Stratmann came out of her office. Molly and Alicia stood close behind Shirley, watching.

The security guard sank onto a chair, trying to catch his breath. "The ring," he managed to say. "The ring—it's gone."

"What?" Ms. Stratmann clapped a hand to her chest.

Everyone headed immediately for the auditorium. It was filled with fading smoke.

Word had gotten around quickly, and soon others were pouring through the auditorium doors. Stink was first, along with his running mate, Bart James, and some of their friends. Bo walked toward Shirley at the front of the stage. Some of the group began to cough and fanned paper in front of their faces. All of them were staring, speechless.

There was the glass display case, empty except for the velvet cushion. The alarm light glowed red.

"I—I was looking right at it!" the security guard stammered. He was still wiping his reddened eyes with his handkerchief. "Then—I don't know what happened! Suddenly there was this smell! And all the smoke . . ."

"I know what it was," Alicia said, pointing at her rival candidate. "A *Stink* bomb!"

"Hey, I didn't do anything!" Stink protested.

Ms. Stratmann studied the display case. "The alarm system—it's still armed," she said. "The light's still on."

"I know," the security guard said. He was breathing more regularly. "It's like that ring vanished into thin air."

Molly Hardy stood with her arms folded across her chest. "What am I supposed to tell my parents?" she asked Ms. Stratmann and the security guard. They looked at her helplessly.

Alicia marched right up to Stink. "It wasn't enough

you nearly electrocuted me, was it, Stink Patterson? If all you can think of to win this election is to play dirty tricks, what kind of president will *you* make?" She looked at the group of kids for support.

"Hey, I'm already winning," Stink said with a grin.

Ms. Stratmann glared at the boy. "Let me tell you, young man, if this is one of your pranks, you can settle it with the police! They'll be here momentarily." She turned her attention to the curious group of bystanders. "Now, I'm sure you all have better places to be, things to do . . ."

The crowd began to break up. Bo stayed at Shirley's side. She was examining the display case and the little cushion.

"What's up?" Bo asked.

"The wiring from the ring case," she said out of the side of her mouth. "Let's follow it."

They slipped backstage, keeping their eyes on the cable. It led to a trapdoor.

"That leads to the basement," Shirley told Bo. She lifted the door by its thick iron ring, revealing a staircase. From her pocket she removed a small but powerful flashlight, which she played over the steps.

"Why am I not surprised this place has a dungeon?" Bo asked, rolling his eyes as they descended.

"Don't worry," Shirley told him. "They stopped using it for detention years ago."

"Huh?"

"Joke," she said, glancing back at him.

"Yeah, well, I'd believe anything weird around this place," Bo said warily.

"This is where the kids hang out while they're waiting to go onstage," Shirley explained. "And they store scenery here."

She moved the flashlight across the floor.

"What's down here?" Bo asked. "What are we looking for?"

"What do you think?" Shirley moved the beam of light to the walls. "Clues. At every crime scene, something is taken and something is left behind."

"Well, we know what was taken. Tell you the truth, I didn't think Stink had it in him!"

"Mmmmm." Shirley aimed her flashlight at a fuse box. She pointed the beam upward and stopped at the top of the wiring leading out of the box. "Look at that," she said.

"What is it?"

"See? It's a digital watch, clipped into the wiring. It's some kind of timer. It could have been used to shut off the alarm on the display case."

Bo stared. "Cool," he whispered.

Shirley made a face at him, and he shrugged. She swung her backpack to the floor and began to rummage through it. *Ah! There it is.* She took out the object and handed it to Bo.

He looked at it and frowned. "Why are you giving me dental floss?" he asked.

"Because," she said, as if he should know, "whoever

set up the timer will be back to get it." She took a camera and a gold box of special film out of her pack. "We'll have to use infrared film," she told him. He watched as she took the dental floss, tied it carefully to the watch timer, and connected it with a dot of sticky putty to the shutter of the camera.

"You can get a picture of whoever comes for the timer?" Bo asked, incredulous.

"When they walk into the dental floss, the shutter will snap." She positioned the camera about four feet away from the timer. She ran her fingers over the grimy floor and rubbed the grime along the floss.

"Can you see it?" she asked.

"Not unless you're looking for it. Now what?"

There was a sudden noise from above. They both looked up, startled by the sounds of voices and heavy footsteps.

"Surely, if you find whoever made the stink bomb . . . ," someone was saying.

"Ms. Stratmann," Shirley whispered.

"Well, the components are easy enough to come by. It could have been anyone," someone replied.

"Inspector Markie," Bo said with a sigh. "I'd know what voice anywhere. So like I said: Now what?"

"Now," Shirley said, hefting her backpack, "we test a theory."

They climbed up the stairs and out the trapdoor. Shirley held her finger to her lips, and they slipped out from stage right, down the side steps, and into the auditorium. The headmistress and Inspector Markie were deep in conversation and didn't notice them.

"I shudder to think what this theft will do to the academy's reputation," Ms. Stratmann was saying. "Nothing like this has ever happened during my tenure."

"Hopefully, we'll have it back before word gets out," the inspector said reassuringly. He looked up and saw Bo.

"Boris Sawchuk," he said, twisting his lips.

"Hi," Bo said.

"What is it about you and crime scenes?" the inspector asked.

"I was just hanging around, hoping to run into you!" he smiled. "And it's Bo, not Boris."

"Aren't you supposed to be in class, young man?" Ms. Stratmann asked.

"Yeah, we were just—" Bo turned, but Shirley was gone. He smiled and shook his head. "Yeah," he said, "I am," and headed up the aisle.

Shirley had hidden behind one of the front pews. She watched the feet of Ms. Stratmann and the inspector.

Ms. Stratmann moved toward the pews and sank heavily into one. Shirley crept over until she was directly behind—and beneath—the headmistress.

"I can't stress the value the Hardy family places on

that ring, Inspector Markie," Ms. Stratmann said as the inspector sat down next to her.

Shirley stared at Ms. Stratmann's feet, but they were flat on the ground. She couldn't see the sole of either shoe.

"Apparently," Ms. Stratmann said, "there was an Earl of Hardy present at the signing . . ."

Shirley thought a moment, then reached into a side pocket of her backpack. She pulled out one of the small brushes she used to collect fingerprints and began to tickle the back of Ms. Stratmann's ankle.

"What signing?" Inspector Markie asked.

Keep sitting, keep talking, Shirley willed.

"Of the Magna Carta! In 1215! It was the dawning of modern democracy!"

The tiny brushstroke made Ms. Stratmann lift her right foot to scratch at her left ankle.

Ah, Shirley breathed, as she took out her magnifying glass. Now she had a perfect view of the shoe's sole.

She studied it, touched it. Not sticky. Except for a few scuff marks, the sole was clean, just as Shirley had thought it would be.

CHAPTER  3

The attic of the Holmeses' big Victorian house was Shirley's favorite place, filled with books and trunks as well as her laboratory, complete with computer, printer, and fax machine.

Bo and Shirley sat back to back at two lab tables. On top of Bo's was a pair of garish yellow-framed sunglasses with a STINK FOR PRESIDENT flag stuck in each hinge. Also on the table was the empty root beer can, still in its plastic bag, and the flyer with the tread marks.

At her table, Shirley was examining an old digital wristwatch. "How'd you get Stink to part with his favorite sunglasses?" she asked Bo without looking up.

"By forgetting to ask," he answered. He began to sprinkle talcum powder on one stem of the glasses. "Okay. It's dusted. Now what?"

Shirley stayed focused on her work. "Now take a piece of tape and lay it over the powder."

"Okay."

"Carefully lift it off."

Bo did, and examined the tape under his lamp. "Hey, it worked!" he cried. "I can see a fingerprint."

"Excellent," Shirley said, and Bo grinned with pride. "Now put it on the transfer card and do the same thing with the root beer can."

Bo placed the tape on a sheet of transparent film and then reached for the bag containing the root beer can.

"Don't forget to wear gloves!" Shirley admonished, still without looking up.

Bo jerked his hand back, turned, and saw she wasn't watching him. He grabbed a pair of latex gloves. "Hey, I'm not totally clueless, y'know," he muttered. He carefully dusted the can.

"Do you like riddles?" Shirley suddenly asked.

"Not much."

Shirley ignored his answer. "What do Alicia's electrocution and the disappearance of the ring have in common?"

Bo turned around in his chair. "They were both shocking?" he asked with a broad smile.

Shirley only raised an eyebrow. "Timing!" she told him. "Ms. Stratmann's shoes were clean, but Alicia's were coated in root beer. Therefore, somebody *timed* that root beer to spill after Ms. Stratmann left the mike and before Alicia got to it." Shirley peered at the watch's parts through a magnifying glass. "Just like they timed the ring's alarm system to switch off at a precise moment and then go right back on again," she explained.

Bo was carefully lifting the second set of prints from the soda can. "So what are you saying—it was the same guy?"

Shirley turned around in her chair. "Precisely!" she said.

Bo laid his second piece of tape beside the first on the sheet of transparent film and picked up his own magnifying glass.

"The whirls match!" he announced excitedly.

"That's *whorls*," Shirley corrected.

"Whatever! It means Stink's the perp!" Bo cried.

Shirley got up, still holding the watch, and went to examine the tapes herself. "He's a suspect," she told him, "and so far our list of suspects includes the whole school. And you're right. They match."

"Yep."

She held the watch under Bo's lamp. She thought aloud: "You know . . . it isn't as hard as you'd think to modify these things."

The next morning Shirley's father, Robert Holmes, arose a little earlier than usual. Besides the fact that he had a meeting to attend, he wanted to try to get the morning paper before his daughter grabbed it. Most children were naturally curious, Mr. Holmes thought, but *this* one—well!

He peered out his window. The welcome mat was empty. *I'll never beat her*, he thought. He sighed and went back to the kitchen to start his breakfast.

He jumped as the CD player on the far counter suddenly started to play his favorite symphony. He turned to the coffeemaker, and his jaw dropped as the machine burbled to life before he'd even touched it.

"What the—?"

"Morning, Dad!" Shirley called from the stairs. She entered the kitchen, stuffing newspaper articles into her backpack.

"Good morning, dear. I see you're off early this morning."

"Uh-huh. And you're a little early yourself!"

"Well, I wanted to—"

"I know. Here it is. Sorry." Shirley handed him the newspaper. "See you tonight, Dad!" She kissed him on the cheek and headed out.

"Have a nice day, sweetheart." Mr. Holmes walked to the bread box and took out two slices of whole-wheat bread. Then he noticed that the toaster had just turned on by itself and two slices were already in it.

Approaching the toaster, he spied his old digital watch. It had been patched into the toaster cord.

He heard the front door slam as Shirley left the house. He looked quizzically in her direction and slowly shook his head.

* * *

In the Sussex Academy basement, directly below the auditorium stage, Shirley checked her camera. She smiled with satisfaction. A picture had been taken. *Now we'll see what's going on,* she thought.

Bo stood guard outside the photo lab's darkroom.

"C'mon, Shirley," he muttered out of the side of his mouth. "The bell's gonna ring any minute!"

"I'm finished," Shirley whispered. She stepped out into the hall, holding an enlarged print.

"What did you get?" Bo asked, peering over her shoulder.

"Somebody's sending us a message," Shirley said, showing him the picture.

"Whoa!" Bo cried.

"Exactly my sentiments," Shirley said.

"But—I don't get it." He stared at the photo. "It's a perfect picture of the display case."

"Right."

"And that *ring,* that ruby *ring*—it's right back there, sitting on its pillow!"

"Indeed."

"But that's impossible!" Bo insisted. "We rigged the camera *after* the ring was stolen!" He looked at Shirley's face. She was wearing an odd smile. "This is weird," he said. "What do you look so happy about?"

"Our list of suspects just got shorter," she answered. "And a lot more interesting!"

CHAPTER

Shirley was glad to hear the lunch bell. She had a lot of thinking to do. Almost on autopilot, she followed her fellow students to the cafeteria and stepped into the line for trays and food.

She noticed that Stink had arrived early to take advantage of some extra time to campaign. He had a can of root beer in one hand, and the other was reaching to shake the hand of everyone who passed him. His vice-presidential running mate, Bart, stood next to him, handing out STINK FOR PRESIDENT flyers.

"Listen, everybody!" Stink yelled. "When I'm elected president, the first thing I'm gonna do is put an end to this health-food thing in our cafeteria! Forget about tofu burgers and alfalfa sprouts! I say, *bring back French fries and gravy!*"

There were shouts of "All *right!*" and "Yeah!" from his enthusiastic clique.

Stink was grinning broadly and trying to ignore Bart, who was tugging at his sleeve.

"Listen, Stink," Bart was saying over the noise of Stink's supporters, "how about the promises you made to *me!*"

"What promises?" Stink muttered out of the side of his mouth.

"Come on, Stink!" Bart said angrily. "What about the Astrophysics Club? We had a deal!"

Stink brushed Bart's insistent hand away. "Yeah, yeah," he said, and continued to slap backs and punch shoulders.

Shirley had gotten her food and was on her way to a table when she saw Alicia and Molly emptying their used trays.

"Come *with* me," Alicia was begging Molly.

"You'll be fine," Molly said encouragingly. "I want to be in the classroom to check out public reaction."

The next round of speeches is after lunch, Shirley remembered. *No wonder Alicia is nervous.*

She glanced up as Bo sat down next to her with his own tray. "Check it out," he whispered, pointing. "Stink's got a little something planned."

Stink was watching Alicia and Molly with a mischievous smirk on his face. "Hey, hey!" he crowed. "If it isn't my worthy opponent on her way to warm up my seat for the second round!" He extended his hand to her.

Alicia just glared at him.

"Come on, Alicia. No hard feelings, okay?" he said.

"*I* wouldn't shake his hand," Molly said.

"Yeah, but Alicia's not like that," Stink said. "We've known each other since kindergarten, right, Alicia?" He lowered his head, and a lock of blond hair fell over his brow. "Hey. I mean it, okay?"

Reluctantly Alicia shook Stink's hand, then jumped back, startled, as a hand buzzer zapped her. The group of students around them laughed. Alicia clasped her hands together, a look of horror on her face.

Molly rushed forward. "How *could* you, after all she's been through!" she cried, pulling Alicia away. "Maybe I haven't known her as long as you have, but at least I have manners! And sportsmanship!"

The students exchanged guilty looks. "Low blow, Stink," Bart whispered. Stink made a face.

"Aw, come on, can't you guys take a joke?" Stink said.

Bo got up from the table, concealing something in his sleeve. As he approached Stink, he slid it out: Stink's yellow sunglasses with the campaign flags in the hinges. "Cool move, Stink," Bo said, and stuck the glasses on Stink's face. "You left these in the can." He turned on his heel and went back to the table.

Shirley took a sip of skim milk. "I've been thinking," she said to Bo, "about that photograph. It's the work of a genius."

"How so?"

"Whoever took it had to put the ring back in the case just for the picture, and then rig the camera again so that we wouldn't notice."

Bo watched Stink parading around the cafeteria, wearing his sunglasses.

"A genius, huh?" he said. "Guess that eliminates Stink."

They sat for a moment in silence, Shirley's eyes taking in the room, Bo's watching Molly Hardy, who had entered with an armful of posters.

Molly was a take-charge kind of person, Bo observed, the kind other people seemed to follow. She looked so confident. *What makes some people leaders and other people followers?* he wondered. He watched some kids call Molly to come and sit at their table.

"Okay," Molly told them. "I just need to put these posters up first."

Bo stood and moved quickly to help Molly with the stepladder.

"Thanks," Molly said with a smile.

"No problem," Bo replied.

Shirley was watching them as she heard a chair scrape on the floor next to her.

Bart sat down, slapping his tray so hard on the table that his soup spilled. He sat and looked at his plate without eating anything. His wire-framed glasses slid down his nose, and he flicked them back into place. His face was red.

"What's the matter, Bart?" Shirley asked pleasantly.

"*Stink's* the matter," Bart snarled.

"What did he do?"

"We had a deal," Bart told her. "I let him talk me into being his running mate instead of running for president myself."

Shirley nodded. "In exchange for . . . ?"

"In exchange for a lot of stuff someone like Stink can do easier than I can. Like, he was supposed to push for more club funding. So have you heard even a single *word* about the Astrophysics Club? The Telemetry Club? The Robotics Club? Huh?"

Shirley didn't answer. She just sat, staring at Bart.

"So *have* you?" Bart repeated.

"I gotta go," Shirley said, and stood up with her tray. She passed Bo, who was thumbtacking a poster into place, and leaned toward him.

"Science room!" she whispered.

He watched as she dumped her tray and hurried out of the cafeteria.

"Science room," he sighed, and followed.

They passed Alicia in the hall as she was on the way into the audiovisual room.

"Good luck," Bo said. Alicia nodded. She barely noticed them. She was trying to calm herself. It was hard enough running for political office without all these dirty tricks!

She closed the door of the broadcast booth and settled herself in front of the microphone. At least she was sitting down this time and didn't have to touch a mike stand! She began to sort through the pages of her speech.

"Alicia?" someone said. It was the technician in the control booth. He was tapping on its window with a pencil. "Are you ready to start?"

Nervously she nodded.

"Okay . . . you're good to go!" He pointed at her with his pencil.

"Hi, everybody," Alicia began uncertainly. "This is Alicia Gianelli. May I have everyone's attention?"

CHAPTER  5

Shirley and Bo could hear the speech being broadcast over the public-address system, but they were busy searching. At least Shirley was. Bo wasn't exactly sure what they were looking for but followed gamely.

"I'd like to talk about some issues I feel very strongly about," Alicia's voice continued from a speaker above them on the wall. "These are issues that affect us all. I'm speaking of the three R's: reduce, reuse, and recycle! No matter what some candidates may think, I believe that Sussex students care about more important things than what the cafeteria serves for lunch!"

Shirley poked around. There were so many hiding places! The science room was full of shelves, cupboards, cabinets, drawers, and boxes. The room had state-of-the-art laboratory equipment, but this time none of it interested Shirley.

Bo was becoming exasperated. "What exactly am I supposed to find here?" he asked Shirley.

Shirley took from her pocket the STINK FOR PRESIDENT flyer they had found the day Election Week began—the day Alicia Gianelli had been hurt.

"Remember this?" Shirley asked. "Remember these tiny tread marks?"

"Yeah . . . sure."

"Well, we're looking for prints that match them." She reached under a hanging shelf and hauled out a cardboard box filled with metal and plastic robots.

"Toys?" Bo asked.

"Robots. Look at their feet. My guess is that one of these robots was used to tip over that can of root beer at a specific time: when Alicia was ready to make her speech."

"Hey," Bo said, frowning. "You thinking of *Bart?*"

"He knows electronics," Shirley said. "He *loves* electronics! And Stink hasn't talked about raising money for the science clubs like he promised he would."

"So?"

"So! He has motive!" She held up her forefinger. "One, he gets even with Stink by framing him with the root beer, the flyer . . ."

"And?" Bo said.

"*And!*" She touched her index finger to make point number two: "Who gets to be president if Stink is out of the way?"

"Oh, yeah!" Bo said as it dawned on him. But Shirley had found what she wanted and dug it out of the box.

"This one," she said, holding up a red-and-yellow plastic robot against the paper flyer. "Its feet are a perfect match."

Alicia's voice on the PA system had been background noise for Shirley and Bo, but both of them noticed a sudden change in her tone.

". . . And there's a lot more I want to do as president," Alicia announced, but her voice seemed angrier. "For starters, let's get rid of some of the *deadwood on the teaching staff!*"

"Did I just hear what I think I heard?" Bo asked. He and Shirley stared at the speaker.

"Better yet, let's just *torch the whole school! Get a modern, new building!*"

Shirley's jaw dropped.

Inside the broadcast booth, Alicia sat stunned. She wasn't speaking, but that was her voice going out over the air to the whole school! It was some kind of recording she had never made. *Where did the technician go?* she wondered. She couldn't see him in the control booth. Once he'd taken care of the setup, he'd probably just left. Alicia tried to turn the mike off, but she didn't know how, and whoever was using her voice continued an outrageous tirade over the PA system. Frantically she rushed to the booth's door, but the knob came off in her hand.

Alicia was in a full panic now. Tears streamed down her cheeks. "Help!" she cried. "Please! Help me!" She pounded on the glass as the recorded voice screamed, " *'Cause it's gonna be ashes to ashes, dust to dust! And we'll all be free! Free!*"

A crowd had begun to gather in front of the door of the audio booth. They could see Alicia's tearful face behind the glass, but no one could get inside. Stink and Bart were there, ready for Stink's turn to speak, and Molly had come running from the cafeteria when Alicia's strange outburst had begun.

When Alicia saw people arriving, she began to pound on the door with her fists.

"It's all right, Alicia," Molly said, "we're going to get you out. Try to calm down."

"Don't break the glass, Alicia," someone yelled. "You'll cut yourself."

Bo and Shirley arrived from the science room with the robot tucked inside Shirley's backpack.

"If Alicia's inside there crying," Bo said, "who's the voice on the PA?"

"It's a recording," Shirley said. "Watch."

Alicia's voice continued to blast over the PA system. "*C'mon, everybody! Let's rock and roll! This is one school that needs liberating!*"

Molly bent down to examine the keyhole on the door.

Alicia's voice shrieked from the speakers. "*And while we're at it, why don't we clamp a muzzle on that old windbag Stratmann!*"

As if on cue, all eyes turned to see the headmistress, who was now standing in the doorway of the audiovisual room. Students bit their lips, students coughed—anything to keep from laughing. Ms. Stratmann's face was even more grim than usual.

"Just what is going on here?" she demanded. She pointed to the door. "What is Alicia doing in there? What is this horrible outrage coming over the public-address system? *I want some answers right now!*"

Molly came forward. "Alicia's locked in, Ms. Stratmann—"

The headmistress cut her off. "Then why isn't someone going for the janitor?"

Molly held up both hands. "It's all right," she said gently. "All I need is a hairpin."

"A what?" Ms. Stratmann glowered at her.

"Please, Ms. Stratmann, I just need one of your hairpins. This is a safety lock"—she gestured toward the door—"and it can be opened from the outside."

Ms. Stratmann fished in the bun of hair at the nape of her neck and handed Molly one of her hairpins. Molly bent down, inserted the hairpin into the lock, and with two twists, popped the lock on the door. Alicia burst out of the audio booth, falling headlong into Molly, who barely kept her balance.

"That's not me!" Alicia cried. "That's not me! I swear, it's not!"

"Of course it isn't," Molly said. The shrill voice on

the recording played on: "*Hey! How about making teachers pay a fine every time they bore us to death!*"

Shirley slipped past the group and into the audio booth. She looked at the control panel for a moment, then flipped a switch, cutting off the PA system. She stood for a moment, looking around.

The group outside had grown calmer. Alicia was wiping her eyes.

Ms. Stratmann looked more bewildered than angry. "Will someone please explain to me what's going on?"

Alicia took a last swipe at her tear-streaked face. "Ask him!" she said defiantly, pointing at Stink.

"Hey! Why does everybody always assume it's me?" Stink whined.

Alicia grabbed Stink's right hand and pushed it against his forehead. The zapper he was carrying buzzed loudly.

"Gee!" Alicia snapped. "I don't have a clue why everyone assumes it's you!"

"Now, that's enough!" Ms. Stratmann said firmly. "I have had quite enough, do you understand?"

The talking stopped. Everyone stood still.

The headmistress folded her arms across her chest. "Candidates," she said, "I want to have a word with you right now!" She turned to the group. "The rest of you: I'm sure you have more important things to be doing!" She waved her arms, shooing them away from the audiovisual room.

"Listen, Gianelli, I didn't do it!" Stink snarled.

"Oh, yeah, right!" Alicia snapped back.

Bo was in the crowd that was moving out into the hall. *Now where'd Shirley go?* he wondered, but she was nowhere to be found. *How does she do that?* he asked himself.

CHAPTER  6

Shirley was on her hands and knees underneath the control panel. She had her mini-flashlight in her mouth and beamed it around the floor as she crawled.

She found what she was looking for in a corner behind a block of Styrofoam soundproofing: a small tape recorder rigged with another homemade timer taped to the underside of the countertop. Shirley put on her latex gloves and removed the cassette from the machine. As she slipped the tape into her pocket, she heard voices in the AV room, so she stayed right where she was.

Right outside the door, Ms. Stratmann was glaring at Stink.

"Never in all my years at Sussex have I witnessed such a disgraceful campaign! Muckraking, backstabbing, thievery—"

"Ms. Stratmann—" Molly interrupted.

Ms. Stratmann cut her off. "Molly, I don't know what you must think of us. Your very first year here, and look what has been going on!" She turned back to Stink. "Mr. Patterson: In the interest of maintaining some shred of decorum, I am going to ask you to step down."

Stink flung his arms into the air. "I'm being framed!" he cried. "You've got no proof any of this stuff was done by me!"

"I'm sorry, but Mr. James will have to run in your place."

Bart raised a fist. "Yes!" he cried. "Bartholomew James for president!"

Alicia turned to Bart. "Congratulations, Bart," she said. "You win. Because I quit!"

"Oh, this is just terrific," Stink sneered. He strode off down the hall.

Bart grinned broadly. "You mean I'm president? Just like that?" he asked incredulously.

"Just like that," Alicia said, and nodded.

"Wait a minute," Molly said. "Just wait one minute here!"

"I'm sorry, Molly." Alicia touched her friend's arm.

"Alicia, you can't give in to scare tactics!" Molly insisted. "Quitting is wrong!"

Alicia sighed. "I've just had enough," she said.

"But what have we been talking about through the whole campaign?" Molly urged. "Isn't democracy worth fighting for?"

"I've *been* fighting," Alicia said, "and I've fought as much as I can. Molly, why don't you run? You'd make a great president."

Ms. Stratmann had been looking from one girl to the other. At Alicia's suggestion, her expression lightened.

Alicia looked at Molly, almost daring her. "Unless," she said, "you're afraid too."

"Of course I'm afraid!" Molly said. "Who wouldn't be, with everything that's been going on here?"

Alicia pulled back her shoulders. "You just said it yourself: Democracy's worth fighting for!" She looked at Molly with hope and admiration.

"Well . . ." Molly bit her lower lip. "Okay. Okay, I'll do it."

"Hey, wait a minute!" Bart said. "I thought we all agreed *I* was president!" He glowered at Molly.

"We're talking about democracy, Mr. James," Ms. Stratmann told him. "You wouldn't want to be president by default, now, would you?" She turned to Alicia and Molly. "Bravo, girls. Well done." She looked up to see Shirley standing in the doorway of the control booth.

"Ms. Holmes?" she said sternly.

"Nothing, Ms. Stratmann. I have class now." Shirley walked past the little group and left the AV room.

* * *

"And what project is this you've been working on?" Gran asked Shirley and Bo, passing a serving dish of broccoli to Bo. He took it awkwardly and passed it to Shirley's father.

"Oh," Bo said, "it's just a—"

"It's a science project," Shirley said. She took the broccoli dish from her father and spooned some onto Bo's plate. "Electricity."

"Mmmm?" Mr. Holmes asked. "Go on."

"Modifying sound," Shirley said. "Eat it, Bo, it's healthy."

Bo curled his lip at her.

"It was lovely that you could come for dinner, Bo," Gran told him. "We so enjoy having you."

"Thank you, ma'am. I guess I've been here, um, a lot, huh?"

"Nonsense," Gran said. "You're a very nice young man and we're always glad to see you. Shirley's right, try the broccoli."

"Sure," Bo said, and gingerly forked a spear.

"How about some Tai Chi exercises after dinner?" Gran asked. "Of course, we should wait awhile, to digest."

"If we get our work done in time, Gran," Shirley said.

Bo glanced around to make sure he wasn't being watched. He reached under the table with a handful of broccoli.

The Holmeses' large basset hound, Watson, pushed against Bo's knee and sniffed the broccoli. Then he snorted and lay down again at Shirley's feet.

"Traitor," Bo whispered. Now he was stuck with a fistful of broccoli, which he stuffed into the side pocket of his slacks. *Rats*, he thought.

After a dessert of apple pie and vanilla ice cream, Mr. Holmes retired to his study, Gran to her apartment, and Shirley and Bo to the attic lab.

"Want me to put on the tape now?" Bo asked.

"Yes, put it on. But first you'd better get that broccoli out of your pocket."

Bo rolled his eyes, then cleaned out his pocket with a paper towel. "Nothing gets past you, does it?" he asked. He clicked the tape into the tape player.

"Now, sit down here." Shirley went over to the computer and pulled up an extra chair. She propped up the photo of the ruby ring against the monitor and began to type on the keyboard.

Soon the sound of Alicia's voice filled the room.

"We could blow up the toilets and flood the school! Water, water everywhere! Hey, wouldn't you like to see old Stratmann doing the dog paddle?"

"Whoa!" Bo said, sitting next to Shirley at the computer. "Talk about venting your feelings!"

"Listen," Shirley said. There were waves on the computer screen. As Shirley worked the computer program, the waves fluctuated and Alicia's voice on the tape got deeper.

"Hey," Bo said.

"Now listen." Shirley made the waves tighter, and Alicia's voice rose.

"It's not Alicia," she said, "but it's a good imitation. It's been modified by a digital program to make it sound like her. It's really not that complicated for anybody with a computer and a sound board."

Bo was frowning. "Yeah, but Alicia was alone in the broadcast booth. How did the tape take over?"

Shirley smiled. "Same M.O. as before: a rigged timer. It was hooked into the audio control board to make the tape cut in."

"Jeez," Bo said, shaking his head. "Bart James always seemed so—y'know—so straight."

Shirley continued to manipulate the recording with the computer. Alicia's voice turned into a deep, masculine sound, then into a piping, squeaky noise.

"But then again, swimming in swill is probably too good for Stratmann," the voice went on.

Shirley was staring at the waves, still working them. "If we can just find the right frequency," she muttered, "we'll find our Einstein."

The tape continued to play in various ranges of sound. *"May—be—we—should—take—her—prisoner—andputherontrial!"* Deeper, higher, faster, slower went the voice.

"How will we know it's him?" Bo asked.

"Bart? Because we'll recognize his voice," Shirley answered, still modulating the tape. Suddenly there *was* a voice they both identified immediately. They looked at each other in stunned silence.

"Wouldn't it be wicked to see old Stratmann begging for mercy? And will we give her any? Not!" the voice chortled.

"Molly?" Bo and Shirley both said at once.

CHAPTER

The next morning—Election Day at last!

Shirley and Bo met near the park and walked to school together. Shirley wore one of her favorite scarves tied around her waist as a skirt, a beige vest with large buttons over a sweatshirt, and a pink cap. Bo had on jeans and a T-shirt with a flannel shirt tied around his waist. This was one of the rare occasions when uniforms were not required. There was to be a picnic, with games and a barbecue on the front lawn of the school. The candidates would give their final rallying speeches, and then everyone would go inside to vote.

Bo thought about the tape from the night before and shook his head. "It can't be Molly," he said. "If you'd kept fiddling with that tape, you could have made it sound like anybody."

"Not someone we know, Bo," Shirley told him. "Look at what's happened in just the past few days:

Molly Hardy's gone from being New Kid Nobody to the most popular kid in school!"

"So?"

They stood together at the edge of the lawn, watching all the students enjoying themselves, feeling so free in their casual clothes.

"Think, Bo!" Shirley said, turning to him. "Alicia's electrocution. The voice recording. It's a classic strategy! Molly created crises to make herself look like a hero."

"But—but that's so *psycho*!" Bo cried.

"Shhh!" Shirley hissed as a few heads turned in their direction.

"Anyway, what about the ring?" Bo asked. "You're saying she stole her own ring?"

Shirley smiled. "Ah, the ring," she said. "Recovering the ring will be her crowning achievement. She'll get to save the school's reputation *and* earn Stratmann's undying gratitude."

Bo looked completely bewildered. "How's she gonna do that?" he asked.

"Remember 'timing'? She's saving that little event for optimum effect. And what better timing than today?"

There was a large homemade banner proclaiming ELECTION DAY tied onto poles near the school's front entrance. There were campaign banners, streamers, and balloons, along with several barbecue grills. The staff had set up tables and covered them with crepe paper bunting. Passersby pointed and commented. Sussex Academy was all dressed up for one of its most festive occasions.

"All we need is a parade," Bo said, looking ahead to where Bart James had climbed on a step stool and begun speaking.

Bart said to the small crowd, "Fellow students, If I'm elected, I promise to raise funds for a satellite transmission dish for the UFO Club! Just think about it! The students of Sussex Academy, broadcasting our very own messages into deep space!"

Shirley tugged at Bo's sleeve and gestured toward the opposite end of the lawn, where Molly Hardy was also speaking. Her audience was larger and more enthusiastic than Bart's. Shirley noticed that Molly was wearing a skirt. No jeans for her.

"Let's hear what she has to say," Shirley whispered with a shrug, and she and Bo moved closer.

". . . And although I've only been at Sussex for a few weeks, what strikes me is the unrealized potential for greater student participation in decisions that affect our future!" Molly was declaring. "With Ms. Stratmann's permission, of course."

Bo rolled his eyes, and he and Shirley glanced at Ms. Stratmann, nodding supportively in the crowd.

"Man, does she have Stratmann in the palm of her hand," Bo said.

"All part of the master plan," Shirley said with a small smile.

Alicia stood below Molly's step stool, waving a MOLLY HARDY FOR PRESIDENT banner and applauding after each sentence.

"In conclusion," Molly went on, "I want to promise you that I will make your concerns heard! You have my pledge that as your president, my voice will be your voice! Thank you!"

She stepped down to enthusiastic cheers and applause. Ms. Stratmann came forward.

"Just a reminder," she shouted over the ovation, "the polling booths will open promptly at noon! Don't forget to vote while you're enjoying the festivities. Thank you."

Alicia trotted off toward one of the barbecue grills, passing Bo and Shirley on her way. "Isn't Molly just amazing?" she asked Shirley.

"Unbelievable," Shirley acknowledged.

Molly walked through the crowd, smiling and shaking hands. Shirley stepped toward her.

"Good speech," she said.

"Thanks." Molly smiled.

"I find it comforting to know your voice will be my voice," Shirley said. "*And* Alicia's."

Molly's smile froze for a beat. Then she broadened it. "I'll do my best to speak for everyone," she said.

Shirley stood her ground. "Just what King John said when he was forced to sign the Magna Carta. You know, legend has it that he pledged the ruby to the nobles as a sign of good faith."

"That's right," Molly said, "and then proceeded to take his revenge on those nobles in every way he could." She and Shirley looked at each other. Another beat. "Now, if you'll excuse me . . ." Molly brushed past her.

Shirley watched her go. *What's Molly up to?* she wondered.

CHAPTER

The smell of hot dogs, burgers, and barbecued ribs filled the air, but it was still early for lunch. While the staff worked to get everything ready, there were games: all kinds of races, touch football, and one-on-one basketball.

Shirley and Bo sat together on the sidelines of an egg-and-spoon relay race. Molly and Alicia, on the same team, were laughing and screaming as they tried to shift an egg from one spoon to another.

Shirley's and Bo's positions were identical: crosslegged on a bench with chins propped up on their elbows. They were both watching Molly like a hawk. Occasionally Bo's eyes would wander toward one of the barbecue grills.

Alicia and Molly made a successful transfer of their egg, and Alicia hurried off toward the next player. Molly, finished with her part for the moment, turned and saw Shirley's grim expression. Molly's smile wavered, but only for a second, as she turned to cheer for Alicia on the other side of the line.

"They're signaling that the food's ready," Bo said. "Aren't you starving? *I* am. Besides," he said, jerking his chin toward Molly, "she's just been playing the games all morning."

Shirley shook her head, her eyes still fixed on Molly. "You go," she told him. "I've got her covered."

"Okay. Want me to bring you something back?"

"No, thanks."

Bo got up and headed for the nearest grill. Shirley stayed where she was, staring. She felt a tap on her shoulder.

"Oh!" She looked up. "Hi, Bart."

"Hi, Shirley." Bart was holding a plate filled with ribs, rolls, and potato salad, and he had a clipboard under his arm. "I was wondering," he said with a shy smile, "if I could count on your vote today."

"Sure," she told him.

"Great!" He put his plate down on the bench next to her and looked at his clipboard. "That makes"—he ticked it off with a pencil—"fifteen!"

Shirley had been distracted for only seconds, but when she looked up again, Molly was gone! She stood and craned her neck, peering at faces through the crowd.

No Molly.

Shirley began to push her way through groups of students until she found Bo on line at one of the food tables. A staff member was placing a hot dog on his paper plate.

"I lost her!" Shirley said.

Bo slathered mustard on his hot dog. "What do you mean, you lost her?" he asked.

"I mean: *I lost her!*"

Bo took a huge bite of hot dog and bun, leaving a mustard smear along his cheek. Wiping it with a napkin, he gazed around the front lawn. "Mmmph," he grunted, his mouth full. "She's right over there!" He gestured with an elbow.

Shirley whirled around. Molly was coming out of the school building, and Alicia was running toward her with some strips of cloth.

"She was probably voting," Bo said, "and now she's gonna be in the race." He polished off the hot dog and reached for another.

"The three-legged race!" Shirley exclaimed, snapping her fingers. "That's what the strips are for—to tie their legs together! Come on, Bo." She turned and began to walk briskly toward the pile of torn cloth bands.

Bo mashed the hot dog into his mouth and followed. "What are we doing?" he managed to ask while chewing.

"We're entering the race." Shirley tied their legs together and dragged Bo to the starting line, where some of the contestants were already in place.

"Partners for the three-legged race should be at the starting line now," a teacher called. "You're going to do four laps of the track, so make sure those strips of cloth are tied tightly enough to hold!"

Molly glanced at Shirley. "Good luck," she said with a smile.

"On your mark," the teacher said.

There was a commotion in the crowd behind them.

"Hey, what's going on?" Bo asked, turning.

"Get set," the teacher said.

One of the boys grabbed Bo's shoulder. "The cops are here!" he said. "They're searching everybody's lockers, looking for that ring!"

Shirley's eyes widened. Her face wore a horrified look.

"Go!" the teacher cried, and blew the whistle. All the racers began to hobble down the track, except for Shirley and Bo, who made a quick right turn toward the school building.

"Wha— Where are we going?" Bo asked. "The race is over there!"

"I know where it is!" Shirley told him. "The *ring*—I know where it is! Molly wasn't voting in the building before. Now that she knows we know, she's going to frame me the way she did Stink and Alicia. She's going to slip the ring into my locker!"

CHAPTER  9

Shirley and Bo stood in a corner of the hallway in the nearly empty school building. Shirley untied the strips of cloth that bound their legs. A few yards away, Inspector Markie and two uniformed officers made their way down a row of lockers. The inspector read the combination codes from a list, and the officers opened each locker door, searching for the missing ring.

"I can't get to my locker," Shirley whispered. "They'll see me. And if I don't get the ring out, they'll think I stole it."

Bo frowned. "Okay," he said, "leave it to me." He strode down the hall toward the inspector.

"Hey!" he yelled. "You can't do that!" He maneuvered himself behind Inspector Markie and the officers forcing them to turn their backs so that Shirley could slink past them and around the corner.

"Relax, Boris," the inspector said.

"I keep telling you, it's *Bo*," Bo said. "And isn't

opening our lockers some kind of violation of our civil rights?"

Shirley reached her locker and got it open. She began to rummage through it frantically.

"Lockers are not private property," Inspector Markie told Bo. The police officers looked on with amused expressions.

"But it *is* my stuff," Bo complained loudly. "You can't go through my stuff any time you feel like it!"

Inspector Markie shook his head impatiently. "Look," he said, "I don't have time for a debate here."

"Oh yeah?" Bo said. "What happened to 'innocent until proven guilty'? Huh?"

"Nobody's accusing you of anything. Why don't you go back outside and let us—" Inspector Markie stopped suddenly as Shirley bumped into him from behind.

"Oh, gosh, excuse me," she apologized. "I just voted and I was in a rush to get back outside!" Without even a glance at Bo, she headed for the auditorium door.

"Oh . . . hey . . . wait a minute," Bo said to the inspector. "I made a mistake. This isn't even my locker. Never mind." He tipped an imaginary hat to the policemen and followed Shirley.

Ten minutes later Mrs. Fish, the headmistress's secretary, entered the auditorium. She looked around to make sure she was alone, then reached into her purse. She drew out a cigarette and lighter, shot another glance around the room, and gasped.

She couldn't be seeing it! It wasn't possible!

There was the ruby ring, back in its display case, gleaming in the dim light. The alarm, wired to the case, was on.

Mrs. Fish began to scream. "Ms. Stratmann! *Ms. Stratmann!*"

Outside, Molly Hardy and Alicia Gianelli sat at a picnic table with a group of girls. They were all laughing at a joke Molly had told when they noticed the headmistress running toward them across the lawn. She had a broad grin and was waving her hands in the air.

"Molly!" she called. "Oh, Molly!"

Molly got up to meet her.

"Wonderful news!" Ms. Stratmann cried, clasping her hands together. "The ring—it's back in its display case!"

Molly's jaw tightened, but she managed a tentative smile. "You're kidding!" she breathed. "That's—that's great!"

"I'm going to my office now to notify your parents," Ms. Stratmann said, and she left Molly staring after her.

"Hi there."

Molly whirled. Shirley stood behind her, watching as Molly's expression grew surly. "You realize, of course," Molly said, "that you have nothing to link me to the theft of the ring."

"True," Shirley answered calmly. "But I foiled your scheme to be a hero."

"And you'll be punished for that . . . eventually," Molly said with ice in her voice. Then she smiled, spun on her heel, and returned to the others at the picnic table.

Later that afternoon the students of Sussex Academy assembled in the auditorium, tired from their day but laughing and talking together.

Onstage Ms. Stratmann was saying, "Now, if you'll all settle down . . ." She waited for silence. "Young ladies and gentlemen, without further ado, I'd like to introduce to you your new student council president: *Molly Hardy!*"

The applause was overwhelmingly enthusiastic. Molly hurried to the stage and shook Ms. Stratmann's hand. She beamed as she gazed out at her cheering classmates, but her eyes fixed on one who was not clapping or smiling.

Shirley returned Molly's gaze with equal intensity. Shirley had no hard evidence that Molly had set everyone up and stolen the ring, but she knew Molly was the criminal even if no one else but Bo did.

Shirley looked at Bo. He looked up at Molly as she made her victory speech and shook his head. "She's scary, isn't she?" he asked.

Shirley nodded.

* * *

That night Shirley sat on her bed. She was in the lotus position Gran had taught her, with her journal open and propped on her legs.

Today, she wrote, *my life has changed in an exceptional way. I have met my equal and my opposite.* She pursed her lips in thought for a moment, then continued: *I wonder if there's room at Sussex Academy for both of us.*